Pretty Young Things

Chase Moore

www.jadedpublications.com

1

    Starr seductively trailed a French manicured finger down the length of Cartier's inner thigh. His muscle instantly tensed up from her intoxicating touch. Wale's *"Diced Pineapple's"* played on low as Starr proceeded to work her magic. She had met Cartier less than thirty minutes ago inside of VIP Lounge on 93rd street.

    The small hood bar was no bigger than the main level of an average sized home, however it usually stayed jam packed. That's how most of the hole in the wall bars in Cleveland was.

    Dozens of fellas had approached Starr that evening. Either they wanted to buy her drinks, spit some pathetic weak ass game, or simply compliment her flawless beauty. However, none had quite caught her attention like the young, hood rich Cartier had. It wasn't even his looks that had initially drew him to Starr—although he was indeed fine as hell with smooth caramel skin, piercing hazel eyes, and a low haircut rippled with jet black waves. The moment Cartier had swaggered over towards Starr she knew without a doubt that she was leaving the club with him.

Dressed in a long sleeve designer shirt, crisp black Levis, and sporting a $150 Paislee Yen Dollar Pout Snapback she was feeling his swag off rip. Starr also noticed the $825 Giuseppe Zanotti sneakers on his feet. *Official*, that was the first thing that came to mind. He was the flyest dude in the club thus far, and he knew it. Fellas had been in her ear all night whispering sweet nothings, but she paid the attention and flirtation no mind. After all, Starr was used to the overwhelming amount of attention she received.

Twenty-one-year-old Starr Renee Coleman was a bad bitch in every sense of the phrase and she knew it. She also used the shit to her advantage. Starr wasn't a cocky female, but she was fully aware of and acknowledged the gift that God had given her: her looks.

People often told her that she reminded them of model/actress Lashontae Heckard, and had even approached her on a few occasions for an autograph.

Cartier wet his lips as he stared lustfully at Starr. Her small, soft hand slowly found their way inside his jeans, and she slowly stroked his dick. She knew just how to touch a nigga. Starr used her sex appeal as she bit her bottom lip seductively and delicately caressed his scrotum.

Feels better when you let it off, don't it...

Know it's easy to get caught up in the moment...

When you say it cuz you mad...

Then you take it all back...

Then we fuck all night...

'Til things get right...

"*Mmm*, Cartier moaned. "Damn, girl...you got me hard as fuck..." He eased his legs wider for better access. "Why don't you get it wet," he said before reaching over and placing his hand on the back of Starr's head.

She offered a girlish grin, and slowly extracted the Winterfresh gum she had been chewing on. "I need somewhere to put this," she told him in a flirtatious tone.

Cartier surprised her when he slowly parted his lips beckoning for her to place the gum there.

Starr giggled. "You on some real freak shit ain't you?" she flirted.

Cartier licked and sucked seductively on her index finger after she placed the gum inside his mouth.

"Bitch, you know you like that shit," he said casually. "Come on and suck on this dick for me..."

Starr tossed her jet black, wavy Malaysian hair over her shoulder. "Can you roll the window down for me first?" she asked. "It's hot as hell in this bitch."

Cartier hit the power button that lowered the driver's side window. It was actually a bit warm inside his custom gun metal black 2013 Cadillac CTS-V coupe. A swift breeze instantly blew inside the car the moment the window was lowered a few inches.

"That's good?" he asked. "You straight now?"

"Yeah," Starr answered with a cute dimpled smile. "Thanks." She slowly lowered her head towards his lap, making sure to keep her hair out of the way.

Cartier reclined his head and closed his eyes. The two were completely shameless as they sat parked in his car around the corner from the bar.

Before Starr's lips could even touch the mushroom shaped head of his dick, the barrel of a 9 mm was suddenly placed against Cartier's temple. He instantly flinched at the sensation of the cold steel.

"The fuck?" he cursed turning towards his left.

A mysterious masked person held a gun against his head through the window as they stood directly beside the driver's door.

With the mask pulled fully over the aggressor's face, Cartier had no idea who the person was, but he damn sure knew what their motive was.

Stevie was a young, light-skinned stud that stood at five feet eight inches tall, and was rather slender in frame. She wore a plain black hooded sweatshirt, and a no-nonsense expression under the black ski mask. Her pink heart shaped lips were full, the corners pulled into a malicious smile behind the mask. Her dark almond shaped eyes were complemented by long, thick lashes. She was sexy as hell even in a boyish sense.

"You know what time it is mufucka! Empty ya pockets and hand over ya jewelry," she demanded in a tone much deeper than her normal voice.

Cartier turned to look at Starr. He could tell from her tone that she wasn't fucking around. However, there was no way he could take her ass serious. Cartier didn't scare easily.

Suddenly, he let out a hearty laugh as if the entire situation was comical to him. "Ya'll mothafuckas is funny man," he said nonchalantly. He was totally unfazed by the entire dilemma.

Stevie instantly looked offended by his unexpected reaction. She couldn't believe this fool had the nerve to be laughing.

"Funny?!" she repeated in disbelief. "Nigga, you ain't in the mufuckin' situation right now to be laughin' at death! And you damn sure ain't gon' think shit's funny when I pull this trigger!" she yelled in a menacing tone. "Now I'ma tell ya ass again. Gimme ya money and je—"

Suddenly, Cartier swung open the driver door instantly slamming it into Stevie's midsection! The gun uncontrollably dropped from her hands as she keeled over in pain. The shit had immediately caught her off guard.

Starr's light brown eyes shot open in their sockets. She didn't see that shit coming at all.

Cartier quickly jumped out of his car in a fit of rage. He was on a mission to teach the two scandalous mothafuckas a lesson. He wasn't the one!

Before Stevie was able to fully recuperate from the blow, Cartier slammed his fist into her jaw.

WHAP!

He had no idea that he had just assaulted a woman and even if he did, he probably still wouldn't have let up. Her ass knew better than to think she could try Cartier. He was a killer and came from a family of killers.

It felt as if the wind had been knocked out of Stevie as she fell backwards onto the asphalt landing with a hard thud. She feared he may have even broken her jaw bone.

"Nigga, you thought shit was really sweet, huh?!" Cartier barked. His fists were still clenched tightly as he stared down at Stevie in anger.

Stevie groaned in pain, and grabbed her jaw as she struggled to stand to her feet. Her entire face throbbed in pain behind the ski mask. She then spit out a small amount of blood from when she had accidentally bitten down on her tongue after Cartier punched her.

WHAM!

Cartier kicked the shit out of Stevie.

"*Oomph!*" Stevie crashed back onto the ground and clutched her injured ribs. "*Aaah,*" she groaned in pain. Cartier was really laying it on her ass.

Starr sat in the passenger seat of Cartier's Cadillac as she watched the entire scene unfold. She felt a combination of fear, shock, and panic. The mixed emotions had her seemingly fastened to her seat, afraid to even move and do something to help her girlfriend.

What did I get myself into, she wondered.

Cartier looked down at Stevie in disgust. Without warning, he slowly unfastened and pulled out the designer leather belt that was previously securing his jeans.

Stevie was lying on her back, holding onto her stomach, and groaning in pain, totally unaware of Cartier's intentions.

Suddenly, he began to viciously assault Stevie with the leather belt making every part of her body a target. He gave new meaning to the term: *whoop that trick!*

Stevie cried out in pain every time the leather belt connected with her body. Even through her clothing that shit hurt badly. She held her hands up to defend herself, but those as well became targets to Cartier's savage beating.

"You thought I was really gon' let yo' punk ass rob me?!" Cartier spat. "*Huh, nigga?!*"

WHAP!

WHAP!

WHAP!

The leather belt repeatedly connected with Stevie's body as Cartier mercilessly beat her.

Unable to withstand witnessing the abuse of Stevie, Starr finally mustered up enough courage, and hopped out of the passenger side. She hurriedly dug into her clutch, and produced a nine inch switch blade. After pulling off and tossing her Loann satin pumps, she charged full speeds towards Cartier who was still beating the shit out of Stevie like a drunken father to his child.

Without warning, Starr jammed the sharp knife into Cartier's upper back!

"Aaaahhh! *SHIT!*" Cartier screamed in pain. A fierce pain shot throughout his entire body as his flesh ripped open from the penetration sharp weapon.

Starr backed away from Cartier as he turned to face her, the knife jutting from his back. It looked like some shit straight out of a Michael Myers movie.

"You...mothafucka..." Spittle flew from Cartier's mouth as he reached for the knife, but quickly decided against pulling it out.

Starr's chest heaved up and down as her heart hammered in her chest. She continued to back from away Cartier. Starr knew that once he got a hold of her it wouldn't be shit nice.

Cartier's gaze instantly shifted from Starr onto the 9mm that lay a few inches from where he stood.

Without a word, he reached down and retrieved the weapon.

Fuck me, Starr said to herself. *What the hell did I let Stevie's ass talk me into?*

She said a silent prayer that if God allowed her to make it out of this alive, she was done sticking niggas up with her girlfriend, Stevie.

God, however, was the last thing on Cartier's mind as he raised the gun towards Starr.

2

WHAP!

Stevie smashed a seven-pound brick against the back of Cartier's head! The gun instantly lowered, but his finger uncontrollably squeezed the trigger.

POP!

A bullet suddenly grazed the side of Starr's bare thigh. The bullet didn't impale her leg, but the damage was enough to draw blood.

"*Aahh!*" Starr cried out in pain, grabbing her injured leg.

Cartier helplessly dropped onto the asphalt. The gun flew several feet from where he landed. He was unconscious before he even hit the ground.

"This motherfucker shot me!" Starr cried in shock and panic. "He shot me!"

Starr's bullet wound was the last thing on Stevie's mind as she stood over Cartier's motionless body. He lay sprawled out on his stomach. Blood gushed from the deep, open wound on the back of his head. Stevie was unsure if he was either dead or alive, but checking his pulse to find out was not something she did not have on her agenda.

Without warning, she viciously brought the brick down onto Cartier's head, instantly caving his skull inward.

She bared her teeth like a madwoman as she slammed the brick down onto his head several more times. Brain matter and bone fragments flew in every which direction as tiny specks of blood splattered onto Stevie's face.

Finally satisfied with the damage she had caused, she dropped the brick and snatched her ski mask off.

Little did Cartier know, Stevie didn't want his damn money or jewelry. Truth be told, she wanted his ass dead.

Starr stared at Stevie in shock and disbelief as she continued to hold onto her thigh. Dark red blood trickled down her leg. She knew Stevie had a temper—after all they had been in a relationship with one another for over four years—but tonight she had witnessed the maniacal side of Stevie. She had seen something in her girl that she had never seen before, and it flat out scared her to death.

This bitch is on some other shit, Stevie thought to herself.

Stevie quickly glanced around her surroundings to ensure that there were no witnesses. "Come on. Help me get this nigga in the trunk," she told Starr.

Starr was in complete disbelief. "I have to go to the hospital," she said. "Are you blind?! I was just fucking shot!"

Stevie cut her eyes at Starr. "Bitch, are you deaf?! I said help me get this mufuckin' nigga in the trunk!"

Not wanting to become Stevie's next victim, Starr quickly limped over towards Cartier's lifeless body and assisted Stevie with the rough task of carrying him over towards the back of the car. After popping the trunk, they tossed Cartier's corpse inside without a hint of compassion or regret.

"Aight, look," Stevie said in a low tone. "This is what we're gonna do...I'ma get in our car, and I want you to follow me in his car. I'ma find somewhere for us to dump this car at," she explained.

"Why do I gotta drive his car?" Starr asked. "Why can't you?"

WHAP!

Stevie slapped the shit out of Starr. "Bitch, ask another stupid ass question, and I'ma fuck you up," she threatened. "Right now I need you to just do what the fuck I tell you." Stevie's expression was serious and no nonsense. Now wasn't the time for Starr to start panicking.

Starr quickly wiped away the blood trickling down from her nostrils. She had unfortunately become accustomed to Stevie's abuse over the years, and was damn near immune to the pain.

"You got that?" Stevie asked. If there was any doubt in Starr's eyes, Stevie damn sure wouldn't hesitate to slap her ass again.

"Yes," Starr mumbled in a tone similar to a child being scolded by its parent. She had her reservations, but now wasn't the time to speak on them.

Stevie's expression softened momentarily. Suddenly, she felt bad. Typical Libra. Stevie could be so damn hot and cold, even in the blink of an eye. "Come here bay," she said in a soothing tone. "I need you to hold it together, aight?" There was a sympathetic expression on her face.

Starr nodded her head in understanding.

Stevie brought Starr's face closer to hers before sliding her tongue inside her mouth. The kiss was rushed and sloppy, however despite everything that was happening at the moment, Starr's clit immediately began to throb.

Stevie quickly pulled away. "Alright, come on. Let's go," she said before running off towards her red 2008 Dodge Charger parked on the opposite side of the street.

Starr hurriedly climbed into the driver seat. "Never the fuck again," she told herself as she started the ignition.

***

Starr sat in the passenger seat and stared straight ahead into the darkness. Even after everything was said and done her heart still pounded ferociously in her chest. Starr's gaze then slowly wandered over towards the side view mirror. Bright orange and yellow flames reflected off the mirror lens. Stevie and Starr had set Cartier's car ablaze only seconds ago with his body still planted inside the trunk. Talk about heartless. She had never done anything this intense in her life, and Starr had her share of the scandalous shit she had pulled in life.

It may have been Starr's mind playing tricks on her, but she could have sworn that she could smell Cartier's flesh burning to a crisp as his own precious car barbecued his ass in the trunk.

Stevie lit a Newport, and took a long drag. She was completely heartless about the shit she had just done. After all, her main goal was to kill

Cartier by the end of the night—unbeknownst to Starr, and she had her reasons why.

Stevie then turned towards Starr and released the smoke through slightly parted lips. Both of her eyebrows had a stylish cut in them similar to the rapper, Souljah Boy's. Stevie raised one of them in questioning. "You know we can't tell nobody about this shit, right?" she said in a low tone.

Starr didn't respond immediately as she continued to stare at the flames in the reflection of the side view mirror. She was in total shock and disbelief about the shit they had just done. *I can't believe we did that*, she kept telling herself.

"Do you hear me?" Stevie asked.

Starr slowly turned to face Stevie. Her lips parted slightly, but she didn't respond. Actually, she didn't know what the hell to say.

Suddenly, Stevie reached over and viciously jammed her thumb inside Starr's flesh wound painfully stretching it open.

"*Aaaah*!!" Starr cried out in pain. Blood gushed from wound as Stevie pressed her thumb deep inside Starr's muscle.

"Bitch, I said did you hear me?!" Stevie spat. She wanted Starr to know that she wasn't fucking around.

"Yes, I heard you!" Starr cried.

Blood continued to spurt out from the bullet wound as Stevie pressed down further. Another inch and she would've punctured Starr's thigh muscle.

Stevie wanted Starr to realize how serious the shit was that they had just done, and Starr being unresponsive had Stevie wondering if she might talk. As a matter of fact, she was actually questioning her girlfriend's loyalty.

Starr had never given Stevie a reason not to trust her, but panic and fear could make a motherfucker say and do anything under the right circumstances.

"I swear! I won't say shit!" Mascara streamed down Starr's cheeks as she cried. Her leg felt as if it were on fire. She couldn't take any more of the pain.

Satisfied with Starr's response, Stevie finally withdrew her bloodied finger. "I'm serious Starr," Stevie said. "Don't tell nobody about this shit—and I mean nobody! *Especially* big mouth assed Diamond."

3

Diamond strutted into Fantasy Gentlemen's Club at approximately 11:30 p.m. A Louis Vutton rolling suitcase was in tow, and a look of determination was on her beautiful brown-skinned face.

Diamond Annette Baker stood at five foot five inches tall and weighed one hundred forty pounds. The twenty-two-year old's hour glass body figure consisted of a pair of 36 D cup breasts and an unrealistically large, ghetto booty—that had been pumped with ass shots on the regular—however, Diamond swore up and down that it was all natural. She was often told that she resembled Toya Carter, and best believe she ate that shit up.

"What can I help you with shawty?" the tall dark-skinned bouncer asked. His gaze wandered over Diamond's frame. She looked sexy as hell in a black contrast mesh yoke dress. The tight dress appeared to be painted on her skin. Her bulging cleavage looked delectable behind the mesh material, and her ass sat upright and beckoned for immediate attention.

A few fellas in the strip club forced their gazes away from the stripper on stage to eye the beautiful brown-skinned woman standing in the doorway. A few dancers tossed envious stares in

Diamond's directions. Their jealousy was no secret. *Who the fuck is this chick walking onto our turf,* were their immediate thoughts.

"I'm here to audition," Diamond said boldly. She held her head high with confidence. One would have thought she was applying for a position for some big-name corporation instead of trying to audition in some hood ass strip club on the east side of Cleveland.

Diamond was the shit and she knew it, and she could give two damns about any hating ass hoes that disagreed or was just plain old insecure about their own average ass looks.

"Auditions ended at nine," he explained, peeling his gaze away from her cleavage in order to look her in the eye.

"Well, can you go and get the owner," Diamond suggested with a slight attitude. "Maybe he'll make an exception for me." Her tone was laced with sarcasm. However, she was dead ass serious.

Diamond knew once the owner got a look at her he would let her audition. He would be a fool not to. Hell, I might even shut shit down, Diamond thought scoping out the competition. There wasn't much if any.

"Aight then," the bouncer told Diamond. "Wait right here," he instructed before walking off to get the owner.

Diamond took another look around the crowded strip club. There was a thick redbone on stage making her ass clap to the beat of French Montana's "*Shout Out*".

The redbone's back was entirely covered with a Chinese dragon tattoo, the tail of the dragon stopped on her left ass cheek. The shit was hot and official.

Let me give a shout out to my real niggas...

Let me give a shout out to my real bitches...

Gon' bust it open for a real nigga...

Singles fluttered in the air as fellas tossed cash much like it was candy. That's just how they got down in Fantasy's.

Fantasy Gentlemen's Club was one of the most popular strip clubs in Cleveland, Ohio. Only the baddest of the baddest females were permitted to dance there, tip out was fairly high at seventy-five dollars, but no dancers made less than a stack even on a bad night.

Diamond's best friend Starr's girlfriend, Stevie had suggested she check out the club. Stevie had said that she frequented the club on the regular and knew how much potential Diamond had to make some serious money. She also told Diamond that she'd be the baddest bitch up in there. Never a nine-to-five kind of chick, Diamond figured it was just the type of convenient cash flow she needed.

Gaming niggas was how she earned her income. Men had afforded her the luxury to eat good, live good, and look good. They kept her bills paid, designer clothes on her back, and even paid the note for her BMW 5 series. However, one could never have too much money in Diamond's opinion, and when her tricks got to cutting up—which they did pretty often—she would have her own money to blow as she pleased.

Diamond looked around the club to see if Stevie was there. She said she might swing through tonight, but Diamond didn't spot her. Knowing Stevie, was probably off somewhere fisting her girl Starr.

Diamond tried to exude confidence, but she wasn't going to front like she wasn't a tad bit nervous. She was hoping Stevie might be there so she could feel a little bit more comfortable but it was what it was, and Diamond damn sure knew better to depend on people. Life had taught her that long ago.

Come on girl, shake that nervous shit off, she coached herself. Diamond had never danced before—other than the strip tease shows she did in the bedroom from time to time—but she figured she pretty much had what it took. She damn sure had the body for it.

"Here she is boss," the bouncer said as he returned.

Diamond quickly pulled herself from her own thoughts as she turned to face the bouncer and the man standing beside him.

Diamond was instantly taken back by the tall, sexy, dark-skinned brother who was obviously the owner of the strip club.

Richard Keys aka "Rich" stood at six feet two inches tall and weighed a solid two hundred and ten pounds. All white everything must have been the motto he stood firmly by hence the white YSL logo t-shirt and crisp white denim jeans he wore. A Burberry belt held his jeans securely around his waist and on his feet were a pair of Louis Vuitton sneakers. On top of his head were a pair of $800 designer sunglasses, and the iced out watch on his wrist and the diamond chain necklace around his neck glimmered in the dimness of the strip club.

He was dark brown-skinned, had a low haircut that was rippled with jet black shiny waves, and a neatly trimmed goatee. Full sleeve tattoos adorned both his arms, and the words "*Rich Boy*" were tattooed in bold cursive lettering on the side of his neck.

"You tryin' to audition?" Rich asked. His deep baritone voice was smooth and melodic. It instantly sent a tingle throughout Diamond's body before settling in between her thighs.

"Yes," Diamond answered.

"What's your name?" Rich asked.

He kept his gaze locked on Diamond's dark brown eyes which were an automatic turn on for her. She was so used to men's eyes roaming all over her body since men rarely if ever offered full eye contact when speaking to her.

"My name's Diamond," she told him before extending her hand. She wanted him to know she was a chick strictly about business.

Rich slowly took her hand and lifted it towards his full lips before placing a soft kiss on the back of it.

He was a regular *smooth operator.* Diamond chuckled in her mind at the funny comparison.

"They call me Rich," he told her. "Well, look here, ma," he said. "The roster's full and these chicks would kill me if I fucked up the rotation. So why don't you come and audition for me in the VIP room."

Diamond's eyes lit up at the mention of VIP. She felt a sudden combination of fear, anxiety, and nervousness. The only VIP she had ever been in was the clubs and bars in the flats and on West 9th.

You got this shit girl, she coached herself.

"Come on follow me," he told her.

Diamond rolled her suitcase along as she followed Rich out of the main entrance of the strip club and down a narrow hallway. The music faded and an entirely different song played in the distance as they neared the VIP room.

Diamond took notice of the way Rich walked. He was swaggering but there was also confidence in his stride like he knew he was just *that nigga.*

"So what do you do?" Rich asked suddenly. "You work a nine to five? You in school or some shit—like most of these girls *claim*?" He didn't even look at her as he spoke.

He had this sexy, nonchalant demeanor about him. Diamond wasn't surprised however. Hell, he owned a strip club. Seeing beautiful women's ass and titties on the regular was the norm for him.

"Um...I do what I gotta do to get my money," Diamond told him. Hell, that's all he needed to know. She was private as hell about what she did for a living, and she had good reason to be that way.

Rich scoffed. "Of course you do. You wouldn't be here if you didn't," he said. He knew the game all too well.

Rich pulled back the black mesh curtain that led into the spacious VIP room.

Rihanna's "*Bandz A Make Her Dance*" remix blared through the speakers. There were a few fellas behind the individual private booths with the curtains pulled. Strippers were providing unrestricted entertainment all for the love of money. Singles scattered the floor as Diamond followed behind Rich.

White and yellow strobe lights reflected around the dim VIP room. Diamond's gaze wandered over towards a booth where the black mesh curtain was slightly drawn. Ole dude was all the way live with his hard dick out and in his hand as he stroked it. With his free hand, he was entertaining himself by fingering the light skinned stripper's asshole.

"Oh, these niggas get too loose back here," Diamond said to herself. Her gaze then wandered down to the large pile of money surrounding the dancer who willingly allowed the man to fondle her ass.

Diamond's eyes lit up at the sight of nothing but twenties, fifties, and hundreds. Hell, for that kind of dough, she was willing to let a nigga stick his tongue in there if he wanted to.

"Come on," Rich ushered snapping Diamond out of a trance.

Diamond followed Rich to a closed black door. She wondered what was behind it. After all, they were already inside the VIP room, right?

Rich opened the door and stepped to the side allowing Diamond entrance first. He then closed the door behind himself.

Diamond anxiously took in the surrounding of the beautiful private room. There was a small stage in the center of the room, and a bar stationed to the left-hand side. Several cozy lounge chairs were scattered throughout the spacious room, and there was beautiful décor throughout including an elegant indoor water fountain.

This nigga gotta have some serious paper to be able to afford all this shit, Diamond thought to herself.

There were no fellas in this part of the VIP room—and Diamond wondered if Rich had it like that on purpose—however, there were three dancers lounging in the room. One of which was on stage slow winding to Rihanna and Future's "*Love Song*".

The other two sat in a chair and sipped on a glass of wine. Diamond figured maybe they were Rich's favorites. After all, why else would they be back here when they could be in the club making money?

"There's a dressing room in the back," Rich motioned towards the door in the farthest corner of the room. "Try to be quick," he added. He said it as if he were on a timely schedule as if he had better things to do.

Diamond was beyond confident, but there was something about Rich that left her feeling nervous. Her stomach churned as she quickly headed to the dressing room.

Once inside Diamond plopped down onto the steel folding chair and unzipped her suitcase. She quickly pulled out a 500 mL bottle of Hennessy. After anxiously screwing off the cap she took a long sip of the cognac until it finally burned her throat.

"*Eeehhh*," she hissed closing her eyes tightly. She took two more quick sips, and then replaced the bottle. "Here we go," she told herself.

4

Diamond slowly made her way into the private VIP room area. Goosebumps instantly formed on her forearms and shoulders. *Damn, get it together bitch*, she told herself.

Diamond wondered if her girl Starr was ever this nervous when it came to sticking niggas up. She knew and respected her girl's hustle. After all it was no secret what she did. Diamond and Starr openly shared their business with each other and there was no judgment passed from either end.

Rich sat carelessly in a lounge chair. One of his "faves" was grinding in his lap while the other stood beside the chair rolling a fat blunt for him.

Ludacris and Kelly Rowland's "*Representin*" played through the speakers. Rich finally peeled his eyes off the female dancer twerking in his lap to get a good look at Diamond. He wanted to see what she was working with.

She looked bad as hell in a turquoise two piece set. Black open toe platform stripper boots complemented her outfit.

Rich instantly sat up in his seat as he eyed Diamond's coke bottle figure. His dick quickly hardened at the sight of her. He tapped the dancer on his lap, motioning for her to get her ass up. Diamond had his undivided attention. The dancer beside him handed him the tightly rolled blunt, and even went as far as to light for him.

They treated Rich like a king, and he was in his own sense. At only thirty-two years old, he had already established legendary street credit. Ex drug lord turned business man, Rich was that nigga. Niggas in the streets feared and respected him, and the ladies absolutely loved him.

He owned Fantasy Gentlemen's Club as well as two bars, one located on the west side of Cleveland and one located downtown.

Rich was both street and book smart which abled him to easily transform his hustle into a more legitimate one. A six-year prison stint had convinced him that he never wanted to end up behind bars again so he did what was best for him, and turned legit having others run the illegal operations he didn't have the time to such as the gun business he had orchestrated for several years.

Diamond strutted over towards Rich. Inside she was nervous as hell, but on the outside, she tried her best to play it cool. Besides, she knew without a doubt that he liked what he saw. He would have to be either gay or blind if he didn't.

Out of the sixty plus dancers on his roster, she was the baddest thing up in Fantasy's and he and Diamond both knew it.

Damn, I want this chick, Rich thought to himself. Instead of thinking about the type of business Diamond could attract to his club he was actually thinking about himself.

Rich nodded his head in approval. He then snapped his finger towards the slender brown skinned dancer on stage and motioned for her to get down.

Damn, this nigga doing it like that, Diamond thought.

"Gon' head. Do ya thing," Rich said. He was a man of few words, and for damn good reasons.

You done took it to a whole 'nother level of freakiness when you blow my mind...

To the point where all the other women kinda feelin' like you to stole they shine...

Diamond slowly made her way towards the stage. Her ass cheeks jiggling with each step she took. Rich loved her stride. He instantly wondered if that pussy was tight. He took a long drag on the blunt. Both dancers leaned on either side of him as they watched and waited to see what Diamond was about to do.

I hope this hoe trips, one thought to herself as she smiled crookedly.

Diamond grabbed the pole and did a cute little twirl around it. The buzz from the liquor had her feeling a little bit more relaxed. She could have looked like an absolute fool, but she would have never known it with the alcohol coursing through her.

Just wanna keep all yo' attention baby...

It turns me on to know I turn you on...

Rich took an aggressive pull on the blunt. He then pulled one of the dancers close enough to kiss her, but instead blew her a shot gun. She seductively inhaled the smoke. He then repeated the motion with the stripper on his right-hand side.

Diamond was getting wetter by the second just from watching the enticing, sensuous gesture from the stage. She wondered if his dick was as big as his ego.

This nigga is hella cocky, she thought to herself. But Diamond would be lying if she said she didn't love a cocky motherfucker. It turned her the hell on.

Who am I kidding, she asked herself. I can't get caught up with a dude like him. Diamond knew better to stick to her lil' tricks instead of flocking to the 'bosses'. They offered less drama.

Rich watched as she did her thing on stage nodding his head along with the mellow beat of the song as he smoked. He looked like every bit of the boss he was.

I will take this chick to a whole 'nother level she's never even seen before, he thought to himself as he watched Diamond perform. Fuck having all the thirsty ass men in the goggling her nude body. Rich knew right then and there that he wanted her all to himself. And he was definitely a man who got what he wanted.

In the middle of the song, Diamond watched as Rich whispered something in the ear of the two dancers on either side of him. Suddenly, all three departed from the room leaving just Rich and Diamond in the privacy of themselves. Oddly enough, she began to get nervous all over again. Her palms were even beginning to sweat as she gripped the metallic pole.

When *"Representin"* finally ended, Trey Songz *"Dive In"* began playing through the speakers. Rich gestured for her to come down and over towards him. He had seen all he needed to see on stage.

Diamond's heart rate sped up as she feared what he would say to her. *I know this dude better let me dance here*, she thought to herself. *I could damn sure use the quick, easy money.*

"How'd I do?" she asked holding her breath until she finally received the verdict.

"I need a lap dance to be for sure if I want you on my team or not," he told her.

Diamond's lips thinned before slightly pulling into a smirk. She turned around and prepared to sit in his lap, but he stopped her before she could take a seat.

"Nah, turn around," he told her. "I wanna see that pretty ass face..."

Diamond offered a girlish grin before she took a seat in his lap. Suddenly one of the dancers returned to the room carrying two stacks of bills. Without a word she handed the money to Rich and left.

He's got these hoes trained like pets, Diamond noticed.

Rich sprinkled singles over Diamond's body as she grinded seductively in his lap. Bills cascaded over her smooth, blemish-free skin.

"You gotta dude?" Rich asked as he stared into Diamond's brown eyes. His expression was that of a serious one as he waited for her response.

Diamond smiled bashfully. "Um...I do me," she said.

It really didn't matter if she did or didn't because he would change that shit immediately if she did. He just wanted to know ahead of time. "Is that a yes or no?" Rich asked. A smile pulled at the corner of his full lips but there was no trace of humor in his eyes.

"Like I said," Diamond began. "I do me..."

Rich stared at Diamond for several seconds as though he were reading her and trying to figure her young ass out. "You know...the truth comes outta bullshit," he told her. "Whether you tell me or not I'ma find out..."

"Why do you care?" Diamond asked in a flirtatious tone.

The two were close enough to kiss each other. Rich's dick was hard in his pants, and Diamond's pussy was wet behind the fabric of her bottoms as she grinded on his erection.

"'Cause I'm likin' what I see and I dig ya attitude, and the way you carry yaself."

"You don't even know me," Diamond teased. However, she wasn't lying. He didn't know her or how scandalous she could be all for the love of money. She was a dime on the outside, but a ratchet hoe at heart.

"Well I damn sure can get to know you," he told her.

"What makes you think I wanna get to know you," she was pushing it, but Rich thought she was fine enough to let talk her shit—to a certain extent.

"It's evident you don't know me, or the type of nigga I am," Rich told Diamond. "Because if you did you'd be honored that I'm even spittin' the shit I am to you right now."

"Someone's cocky," Diamond teased.

"And best believe I've earned the privilege to be this way," he told her. "I'ma confident nigga...and when I want something I get it...and right now I want you—and I'm not talkin' bout just climbin' up in you," he quickly added. "Pussy ain't hard for a nigga like to me obtain," he said. "I mean I want you want you. But first I gotta see how you act."

Diamond wasn't used to a man blowing down on her the way that was Rich was. His aggression coupled with swag had Diamond turned on, but she wasn't ready to let him know all that. Besides, his cocky ass probably already knew the effect that he had on women. She had no intention of giving him the satisfaction of pumping Rich's head up more than it already was.

"So does that mean I'm a part of your team?" Diamond asked changing the subject. She was ready to get down to business and more importantly she was ready to make that gwop. "I can join the roster?"

"Work here?" Rich asked confused. "Hell no."

Diamond looked confused. "So I didn't get hired?" she asked in disbelief.

"Baby girl, you can't even dance on the real," he told her. "The shit you was just doin' up on some stage was some amateur type shit. I got hoes downstairs doing backflips and cartwheels on stage. Are you fuckin' kiddin' me?"

Diamond looked offended, and she damn sure didn't appreciate what she was hearing. She was for certain that she had the audition in a bag. Besides, she was killing the hoes that worked there on the looks side.

"But it's cool," he quickly said noting her disappointment. "I gotta much better and easier job for you...if you want it," he told her.

Diamond stared at Rich cautiously. "And what's that?" she asked curious to know.

"Why don't you go get dressed first?" Rich told her. It was more so a demand than an actual question. She had never met a guy as bossy as him.

Diamond quickly dressed and then rejoined Rich in the private VIP room. He had his iPhone already out and ready to program Diamond's number inside. "Put ya number in here," he told her. He wasn't even giving her an option to turn him down. If she knew what he knew, her ass would be programming her cell number, house phone number, hell, even her mama's number.

After she punched in her cell phone number, he locked in her. "I'ma hit you up," he promised.

"When?" Diamond wanted to know. She needed to make sure that she wasn't preoccupied with one of her many tricks.

"When? I don't know," Rich told her. "I'm a busy man, but just be lookin' for that call from me. I promise you fuck wit' a nigga like me, I'll change ya life. Don't sleep on some real shit ma."

5

Understandably, Diamond was upset that she wasn't able to make money at Fantasy's that night. She had her hopes a little too high, and figured she pretty much had it in the bag the minute she stepped through the doors. Unfortunately, Rich had come along and burst Diamond's "confidence bubble."

Diamond closed and locked the apartment door behind herself. She lived in the luxurious Atrium Apartments located in Beachwood, Ohio.

She wondered what exactly Rich was talking about when he had said he had a job for her.

Shaking the thoughts from her head, she pulled out her Samsung Galaxy S II and called up one of her tricks, Lavelle. He was one of her most loyal clients, and she fucked with him heavy because he was already married, and understood the business exchange they had between them— unlike the many men she messed with who were trying desperately to wife her. Lavelle kept it platonic and strictly business. He bust his nut and kept it moving.

Lavelle was an ole freaky, nasty motherfucker but he paid generously for

Diamond's services and never gave her a hard time.

"What's up?" Diamond greeted. "Is the Misses around?" she asked referring to Lavelle's wife.

There was shuffling on Lavelle's end and silence for a brief moment. Diamond figured Lavelle was probably getting out the bed, and heading to a secluded area in his home so that he could talk to her.

Creeping motherfucker, Diamond thought to herself. She then giggled on her end.

"Hey, what's going on babe?" Lavelle greeted.

"You," Diamond said boldly.

She wasn't beating around the bush with her shit. She wouldn't sleep peacefully at night if she didn't make a certain amount of cash every day. That's the way Diamond was programmed.

Lavelle sighed into the receiver. "Aight...gimme about a half an hour and I'll be over." He knew what time it was.

"I'll be waiting," Diamond stated before disconnecting the call.

She undressed, but didn't even bother showering although she was still a little sweaty from the brief performance she put on for Rich. Lavelle wouldn't mind. He was on some real freak type shit when it came to Diamond.

Forty-five minutes later there was a soft knock on Diamond's door. Lavelle killed Diamond with that shit. She always knew it was him too because he was the only one who did that half assed knock. It was as if he feared she might have a man over or some shit. Hell, he was the one creeping. Not her.

Diamond wore a pink satin robe as she sashayed towards the door. She opened it, and there Lavelle stood looking as handsome as ever. He reminded Diamond of the actor, Malik Yoba, and probably even had the same amount of income. Lavelle was an oral and maxillofacial surgeon who earned well over two hundred thousand dollars a year.

Diamond stepped to the side and allowed Lavelle entrance. He wore a white dress shirt that was half buttoned along with a pair of un-ironed black slacks. Diamond could tell that he had dressed in hastiness.

"You didn't shower, did you?" was Lavelle's first question.

"No...I didn't," Diamond told him.

"Alright then," he said. "You know how I like my 'tang'." Tang was the word he used to describe a woman's natural body scent mingled with a little sweat, and musk. It drove him crazy.

Diamond took Lavelle by the hand and led him towards her bedroom. Once she closed the door behind them she turned to face Lavelle and held her hand out.

Lavelle scoffed, and ran a tongue along his inner cheek. Diamond didn't fuck around with a nigga.

"I didn't stop at the bank before I came here," he said as he fished in his pockets for his wallet.

"And why's that?" Diamond wanted to know.

"I've already withdrew the max," Lavelle told her. "The wife's car needed some major repairs done to it," he explained.

"What's that got to do with me?" Diamond said in a sassy tone. "You can take care of your wife, and then bring ya ass over here and give me what's left?" Diamond asked with an attitude.

Lavelle cut his eyes at Diamond. "Watch it," he warned. She damn sure knew how to push his buttons and his wife was already a touchy subject with him.

Diamond decided to chill out. Besides, she needed her money.

Lavelle fished in his wallet, and handed her a small wad of cash.

Diamond anxiously forked through it. Her eyebrows furrowed as she frowned. "Four hundred bucks?!" she said it as if he had just handed her a twenty-dollar bill.

"That's all I got on me, Diamond," he told her. "Now come on, I'm getting soft over here..." He took Diamond's hand and guided it towards his flaccid penis.

Diamond quickly snatched her hand away. "Nigga this won't even cover my damn car note," she said in a nasty tone. "I hope you wasn't expecting some pussy for this little bit o' ass cash."

Lavelle rolled his eyes. "Fine...I won't fuck you," he said. "But at least let me eat your ass...can I do that?" There was desperation in his voice, and a begging expression on his face.

Diamond pretended to mull it over, but she had already made her mind up pretty much. Real talk, she would've gladly just given him head. She undid her robe and allowed it to fall around her feet. "I guess," she said nonchalantly before walking over towards the bed.

Lavelle looked like a kid on Christmas.

***

"You ain't talkin' to me now?" Stevie asked Starr.

Starr sat on a bar stool at the kitchen island and sipped on a glass of Blackberry Moscato Sangria. The aching pain in her leg had finally subsided after popping two Tylenol and dressing her wound.

The two of them lived together in The Avenue District Apartments near downtown Cleveland. Sticking up niggas afforded them the leisure of renting the luxury apartment. Stevie also assisted in a low-key weapon operation, but didn't get paid nearly as much as she wanted to—partly due to the fact that the greedy nigga who helped run it with her was taking some of her cut.

Stevie sucked her teeth and rolled her eyes once it was evident that Starr wouldn't respond. She figured maybe she had flew off the handle a little bit when she had jammed her finger inside Starr's wound, but she only wanted to get her point across.

Stevie walked over towards Starr. She wore a pair of loose fitting basketball shorts and a fitted white beater. Her small breasts were nearly non-existent, and her short curly hair was partially damp from the shower she had just taken.

Stevie slowly turned the swivel bar stool towards her, and stared deep into Starr's beautiful eyes. "Look, I ain't mean to flip on you, aight?" Stevie said. "About tonight...look, if I wouldn't have did what I did our asses would probably be dead. Shit, I had to do what I had to do," Stevie explained. "For us..."

"Stevie," Starr began in a low tone. "You promise you were done putting your hands on me..."

Stevie released a deep sigh, looked down, and ran her fingers through her short curly hair. "I was panicking, bay. My fault, aight."

Starr nodded her head even though she wasn't buying that half assed apology.

"You love me?" Stevie asked her girl.

"You know I do," Starr told her. "You shouldn't even have to ask." Hell, she had just assisted with murdering a guy and covering up the evidence with Stevie. If that wasn't love, Starr didn't know what was.

"You'll never put a man over me?" Stevie asked.

"Never...I promise."

Stevie pulled Starr close to her and planted a passionate kiss on her lips. She then pulled back and stared into Starr's eyes. "I'll never do you like these niggas out here did you," she promised. "I will die for you girl."

They indulged in another passion-filled kiss before Stevie lowered herself at Starr's waist level. Starr wore only an oversized NFL t-shirt with no panties on underneath.

Stevie slowly spread Starr's legs apart while she sat on the barstool. Starr ran her fingers through Stevie's short curly hair as she buried her head between Starr's thighs.

Stevie flicked her tongue over Starr's throbbing clit in a fast-paced motion.

"*Oooh*, shit," Starr moaned.

Stevie dipped her thick, pink tongue inside Starr's slick opening, devouring her pussy much like she had something to prove. And in a way she did. Stevie wanted Starr to know that there wasn't a nigga in the world that could do what she did.

Starr's cheek's flushed as she spread her legs farther apart. Stevie had that epic tongue game. She put niggas to shame.

"*Mmmhmm*," Stevie moaned as she licked, lapped, and sucked aggressively.

She then pulled away, and slid two fingers inside Starr's drenched pussy.

"*Aahh,*" Starr moaned. "That feels so good," she whimpered.

"Feels good?" Stevie asked. "You gon' cream in my mouth?"

Starr tossed her head back, and bit her bottom lip seductively. "Yes!" She thrust her hips forward and fucked Stevie's fingers.

Stevie quickly replaced her fingers with her tongue French kissing Starr's soaking wet pussy.

Starr bucked and jerked as she felt a powerful climax approaching. She encased her bottom lip and grabbed a handful of Stevie's soft curly hair.

"I'm cumming," she moaned.

Stevie licked and sucked harder.

Starr's orgasm came fast, hard, and strong.

Stevie slowly stood to her feet and wiped away the wetness on her mouth and chin. She then leaned over and planted a soft kiss on Starr's lips.

"I love the way you taste when you cum," Stevie said. "I love you so much baby," she admitted.

"I love you too," Starr said. The response was so programmed that it came out instinctively, but the truth of the matter was, she didn't feel the same way about Stevie that she felt initially.

Starr loved Stevie...but unfortunately she was no longer in love with the controlling, abusive woman.

Stevie turned and headed towards the bedroom. Starr grabbed her cell phone and headed towards the bathroom, closed and locked the door. She then plopped down on the toilet seat and sent her best friend, Diamond a text message that read: *I don't know how much longer I can take dealing with Stevie.*

6

Diamond's cell phone chirped on the nightstand indicating that she had just received a text message. Lavelle had left over an hour ago and she was once again alone in the comforts of her own home.

Diamond reached over and grabbed her iPhone. After unlocking the screen, she realized that Starr had just texted her. She opened the message and quickly read it. Diamond then texted back: *I don't know how much more of this life I can take.*

Diamond and Starr had been best friends ever since their freshmen year in high school. They clicked almost immediately the moment they had met, and had been inseparable ever since. The two friends were both "get money type of broads", who were more street savvy than book smart so both women dropped out of high school, and decided to take a different, much darker route.

Starr, along with her girlfriend, Stevie had been sticking niggas up for years while Diamond used her good looks and body to get any and everything she wanted in life.

Diamond never thought she'd say it, but truthfully she was becoming tired of the same old routine. It would be nice to just have one good man that took care of her, spoiled her, and treated her like a queen.

Diamond's mind then wandered towards Rich. She wondered how soon it would be before he finally called, and what exactly he had in store for her.

***

Rich padded barefoot inside the kitchen the following morning. His attractive Spanish chef Lolita was cooking breakfast—an egg, cheese, sausage, bacon, onion, and green peppers omelet.

"Buenos dias, papi," she greeted.

Rich walked over towards Lolita, planted a soft kiss on her cheek and squeezed her ass. He pretty much dug in that pussy whenever he felt like it.

Lolita offered a girlish giggle. "How'd you sleep?" she asked in her thick Spanish accent thick.

"Pretty good."

Rich took a seat on the kitchen bench located in the farthest corner of the kitchen. Lolita already had his spot prepared just the way he liked it, as she did every morning.

A fresh, hot cup of coffee was positioned next to The Plain Dealer and on top of the newspaper were his cell phone, and a notepad and pen. Rich was a hood nigga, but he could be pretty anal retentive at times.

Steam rose off the top of his coffee mug. Rich was just about to open the newspaper when suddenly his cell phone began ringing.

Gotcha bitch tiptoein' on my marble floors...

Red bottoms only for the centerfold...

Rich recognized the number immediately. It was his right-hand man, Keesh.

"Yo," Rich answered.

"Nigga turn on the mothafuckin' news!" There was urgency in Keesh's voice.

Rich quickly stood to his feet and walked hastily into the living room. After turning on the seventy-three inch Mitsubishi TV, he put on the 19 Action News channel.

"Nigga, ain't that mothafuckin' Cartier's car?!" Keesh yelled into receiver.

The phone suddenly dropped out of Rich's hand and landed onto the polished cherry hardwood floors. The back piece to the phone popped off and the battery disconnected from the cellphone. Rich's mouth fell open as he stared at the television screen.

"*...Developing news on the vehicle that was set ablaze late last night, and the corpse discovered in the trunk of the car...*"

The news reporter's voice seemingly trailed off as Rich stared at the burnt-up vehicle on the screen. His little brother Cartier was the only nigga he knew that had a custom 2013 Cadillac CTS-V coupe. As a matter of fact, Rich had brought it for his brother on his twenty-fifth birthday.

"The f—Nah...nah," Rich told himself clearly in denial. He knew what he was seeing on the news, but his mind fought to believe what he was hearing.

Rich picked up his cell phone and the pieces up from the floor and quickly reassembled it. After powering the phone on, he dialed Cartier's number. Oddly enough, the line sent him straight to Cartier's voice mail.

"*Aye, you reached the nigga Cartier. I'm either busy or just flat out ignoring your ass. Leave a message, and I might get back with you...*"

Rich disconnected the call.

"The fuck is going on?" he asked himself. "Nah...this...this shit ain't happenin'...this gotta be some type of fuckin' mistake."

Rich. decided to dial up Cartier again, but to his dismay was sent straight back to his brother's voicemail.

"Fuck!" Rich hissed. He headed towards his bedroom to change into some clothes and get to the bottom of shit.

"You're not eating breakfast?" Lolita called out after him.

"Fuck that breakfast," Rich spat. The only thing on his mind was seeing what was up with his little brother.

The fact that the car on the news looked much like his brother's car had his nerves on edge, and Cartier's phone sending him straight to voicemail left a bad taste in his mouth. Some shit was definitely not right, but he was about to find out what was up.

7

Knock!

Knock!

Knock!

Knock!

Diamond shuffled in bed and groaned aloud. "*Mmm...*"

Knock!

Knock!

Knock!

Knock!

Diamond snatched the comforter off her body. "I'm coming! I'm coming!" she yelled out in irritation.

She slowly made her way out the bed. Scratching her ass, she walked lazily towards the front door.

"Who is it?" she called out.

"It's me. Open the door," A familiar voice said.

Diamond forked a hand through her disheveled hair, trying to fix it up. She then blew her breath in her hand and smelled it. She wasn't very satisfied with the results. However, she still went ahead and opened the door.

Stephanie Marie Thompson aka Stevie stood in the doorway wearing an expressionless look on her face. She wore a red Adidas hoodie, a loose-fitting pair of Levis, and a red Obey snapback on her head.

"You gon' just stare at me or you gon' let me the fuck in?" Stevie asked with an attitude.

Stevie was used to talking and acting reckless with her girl Starr because Starr allowed that shit. However, Diamond wasn't Starr and she'd be damned if she allowed Stevie to talk greasy to her.

"Check ya attitude at the door mama," Diamond said.

Stevie scoffed and straightened up her posture. "May I come in? Please," she added in emphasis.

Diamond stepped to the side and allowed Stevie entrance. "That's more like it," she smiled.

As soon as Stevie stepped inside she leaned towards Diamond, expecting a kiss.

Diamond planted a quick, half assed peck on Stevie's lips.

"Damn," Stevie said in disappointment. "That's all I get?"

Diamond smiled. "I ain't brushed my teeth yet," she explained.

Stevie shrugged nonchalantly. "So? I don't mind a lil' morning breath," she told Diamond. "Let's me know it's real..."

Diamond had been fucking around with Stevie behind her best friend Starr's back. Initially Diamond had never even been into females herself, but one night of drinking had led to one thing or another, and Stevie ended up at her apartment with her face buried between her thighs.

Diamond didn't have any emotional attachment to Stevie, but she damn sure let her suck on her pussy every now and then. Diamond kind of felt bad about it since Starr was her best friend, but the damage was already done. Starr was happily in love, and Diamond would rather let Starr remain a fool in love than to break her poor heart.

"What's up?" Stevie asked. "So did you check that club out like I told you to?"

Diamond sucked her teeth and padded towards the kitchen. "Yeah, I did," she answered.

"But the *big shot owner* told me I wasn't good enough to work there."

Stevie gasped in shock. "Fuck outta here. Rich said that shit? You would've been the best thing up in that bitch and he knows it."

Diamond opened the refrigerator and pulled out a 20 oz. bottle of Tropicana. She closed the refrigerator door and turned to face Stevie. "Rich...? You say his name like you know him personally," Diamond noted.

"I mean...I uh—I fuck with him on a business tip," Stevie explained. "But I don't know dude personally."

Diamond's eyebrows furrowed. "Business?" she repeated. "And what business do ya'll do together?" she wanted to know.

Stevie walked towards Diamond. "You don't need to worry your pretty lil' head about that," she teased. "All you need to worry about is that dick when I put it up in you."

Diamond took a swig from the orange juice and almost choked on it after hearing what Stevie had said. "Girl bye," Diamond laughed. "You ain't stickin' no plastic up in this pussy."

Stevie crossed her arms over her small breasts. "Bitch, I bet I make you cream on this dildo," she challenged.

"We'll never know," Diamond said. "'Cause you ain't stickin' no fake ass dick up in this. That tongue is good enough for me."

"Oh, this tongue is good enough, huh?" Stevie flirted. "So you're just using me for my tongue now?" She approached Diamond and wrapped her arms around her waist.

"Maybe," Diamond smiled flirtatiously.

Stevie backed Diamond up against the kitchen counter. She then leaned forward, and seductively sucked on Diamond's bottom lip.

Stevie pushed away the containers behind Diamond making more room on the spacious counter. She then helped hoist Diamond up onto the counter.

Diamond giggled as Stevie slowly lifted Diamond's t-shirt over her head before tossing it onto the kitchen floor.

"You love my tongue game, huh?" Stevie asked smiling.

Diamond seductively trailed her tongue along her upper lip. She knew what was coming next. "You know I do," she whispered.

Stevie lowered herself down and slowly worked her way up Diamond's leg, placing soft kisses along her skin. She then began slowly swirling her tongue around the flesh dangerously close to Diamond's pussy.

"Damn Stevie," Diamond moaned in pleasure. "That shit feels good girl," she told her.

Diamond's pussy was dripping wet before Starr's tongue even touched her pierced clit.

"Suck that pussy," Diamond coached Stevie.

She arched her back and thrust her hips into Stevie's face. Stevie sucked gently with expertise on Diamond's swollen clit.

"*Yes, fuck*!" Diamond moaned out in pleasure. She grinded her pussy against Stevie's mouth.

"*Mmmhmm*," Stevie moaned in confidence. She knew just what she was doing when it came to eating pussy and she did that shit like a pro.

Stevie dipped her tongue into Diamond's slick opening, tasting her sweet nectar.

"*Oooh*, shit," Diamond moaned. She immediately ran her fingers through Stevie's soft, short curly hair as her tongue slid in and out of her.

Stevie buried her face further between Diamond thighs French kissing and sucking on her throbbing clitoris. She had no shame after having eaten out the two best friends back to back.

"*Oooohhh,*" Diamond whimpered. "You're gonna make me cum Stevie…"

Her right leg trembled uncontrollably as Diamond licked and sucked aggressively.

Diamond's toes curled as she prepared herself for the approaching orgasm. "I'm…about…to cum," she whispered.

Stevie began to lick faster, and suck harder. Seconds later, Diamond exploded all over Stevie's heart shaped lips and chin.

"Damn," Diamond panted trying to catch her breath. "You did that shit, girl," she smiled.

***

Rich pounded on the front door of his brother's home. His nostrils flared wildly as he impatiently waited for someone to answer the door.

BOOM!

BOOM!

BOOM!

Rich continued to pound on the front door with a closed fist until he finally heard footsteps approach the door.

Seconds later, Cartier's baby mother, Trina opened the door slightly. She was a young, pretty dark skinned chick that looked a lot like actress/ singer Naturi Naughton. There was a surprised and apprehensive look on her face.

"R—Rich," she stuttered. "What are you doing here?"

Rich bombarded his way inside Cartier's home. "Where the fuck my brother at?" he asked.

"Uh...Rich—I...uh—"

"You ain't see the mothafuckin' news?!" he barked at Trina. "They found Cartier's car set on fire in an alley last night. A body was in the trunk."

Suddenly Rich's gaze wandered towards the half-naked brown skinned brother that just emerged from Trina's bedroom. He wore only a pair of plaid Fruit of the Loom boxers. He took one look at Trina and then Rich.

"Who the fuck is this nigga?!" Rich asked in disbelief.

Trina twiddled her fingers as she stared down at her feet.

"I said who is this nigga?!" Rich yelled.

"Man, maybe I should leave," Trina's company said in a nonchalant tone.

Rich suddenly snatched out his Glock and aimed it at the mysterious stranger. "Nigga you must've lost yo' mothafuckin' mind—"

"Rich! *NO!*" Trina screamed before grabbing Rich's arm.

Without warning, Rich smacked Trina in the mouth with the butt of his gun.

She stumbled backwards and crashed onto the carpeted floor of the living room. Blood seeped from the open wound that quickly opened on her lower lip. He had no respect for her trifling ass period, and hated that his brother even got involved with her especially after he used to fuck with her years ago.

"Hoe, you got this nigga up in my mothafuckin' brother's house!" Rich yelled. His heart beat rapidly in his chest. He didn't know what the hell was going on with Cartier, and the fact that Trina had some random nigga in his house had him thinking and behaving irrationally.

Rich turned his attention towards Trina's male friend. He held his hands up defensively, and was damn near on the verge of pissing himself. He closed his eyes and said a silent prayer.

"You would die for this pussy?" Rich asked the guy. He wanted to fuck with him before he pulled the trigger on his ass.

The guy didn't respond immediately. He was to shaken up to reply. Trina cowered and cried in the corner of the living room. She knew how crazy Rich was. She had heard the stories about the heartless things he had done to people in his heyday, and she recalled the few ass whuppings he had laid on her back in the day. Nevertheless, she didn't fully think about the consequences of her getting caught. Trina knew that Cartier did his thing out in the streets so why couldn't she have her piece of dick on the side?

"Nigga, I said would you die for this pussy?" Rich spat.

Trina's friends closed his eyes tightly and expected a bullet to his head at any given moment.

Gotcha bitch tiptoein' on my marble floors...

Red bottoms only for the centerfold...

Rich's cell phone suddenly rang interrupting the tense moment. He pulled out his phone. "Hello?" he asked keeping his gaze locked intensely on Trina's male friend.

"Rich..." It was Lolita. "Some men are here to see you," she said in a low tone.

8

Rich sat at the dining room table and ran a hand over his waves. He released a deep sigh as he struggled to accept the bombshell that had just been dropped on him. It felt like his entire world was crashing down around him.

Ten minutes ago, two detectives had just moseyed into his home and told him that his brother was murdered.

Rich felt shocked, saddened, angered, and half-way still in denial. He had damn near raised the little nigga himself being seven years older, and the police telling him that his flesh and blood was gone had Rich feeling like a part of him had died as well.

This shit isn't happening, he told himself.

Rich knew that Cartier was the type of nigga that liked to floss and stunt, but no one really had a real legitimate reason to kill him. He was a likable cat. He had broken a couple hearts, but Rich doubted a spiteful ass bitch would have a nigga kill Cartier, and Cartier didn't have any beefs that Rich knew about.

Hell, niggas in the street knew better than to fuck with Cartier or else they'd have to step to Rich.

This shit is just not fucking happening,
Rich told himself again.

The detectives had promised to do
everything they could to solve Cartier's murder,
but Rich wouldn't give them a chance to solve
shit. He was definitely planning on taking
matters in his own hands. As a matter of fact, he
was going to have his homeboys and soldiers
find out any and everything they could about
who killed Cartier, and Rich would make their
asses suffer.

Lolita placed a fresh cup of coffee in front
of Rich. She knew how upset he was and she was
simply trying to cheer him up although her effort
was subtle.

Rich immediately flipped the fuck out!
"Get this shit the fuck away from me, man!" he
yelled before knocking the mug of coffee off the
table.

The porcelain mug shattered on the
hardwood floors. Lolita flinched in fear. She
wasn't expecting Rich's reaction at all. Obviously,
he didn't like or appreciate the gesture.

"I'm...I'm sorry," Lolita stammered. "I...I
was...just trying to help—"

"Help?!" Rich repeated. "You wanna know
how you can help me?! The fuck outta my
house!" he yelled.

Lolita didn't have to be told twice as she quickly ran out of the dining room crying.

***

Stevie took a long drag on the cigarette as she sat in her car. Sometimes she liked to just chill in her car in the building's garage. The secluded area allowed her to get a piece of mind, and to just think. Starr also hated when she smoked in the house, arguing that the scent got stuck in the furniture so to keep from hearing her girl's mouth she began smoking in her car.

Stevie turned up the volume to the radio as she listened to the news report about the body found in the trunk of a car. It was Cartier of course.

A smile tugged at Stevie's heart shaped lips. "They gon' have to pull that nigga's dental records to identify his crispy ass," she laughed to herself. "I told that nigga," Stevie said. "I told that nigga not to underestimate me...especially when it comes to my money..."

Stevie worked for Rich. Her and Cartier operated the little gun hustle he had going on. Since Cartier was Rich's brother, he obviously felt that it was okay to dip into Stevie's cut from time to time. She got sick of his greedy ass dipping into her money so unfortunately she had to do what she had to do.

Starr didn't know the details of Stevie's side hustle. Stevie was very vague when it came to that besides it wasn't any of Starr's fucking business in Stevie's opinion.

Last night Starr simply thought that she was setting up some random nigga in the streets, however unbeknownst to her, Stevie had plotted the shit out like clockwork.

Stevie took another pull on the cigarette as she thought back to last night's events.

***

Stevie walked over Cartier and dapped him up. "What's good nigga?" she asked. The phony ass smile she gave him was worthy of an Oscar.

"What's up?" Cartier said.

"Shit, chillin'." Stevie took a swig from her Budweiser. "Damn...who is *that*?" she suddenly asked.

Cartier's gaze followed Stevie's to the fine ass chick wearing a nude panel Bodycon dress at the bar. He had run through most of the hoes in the bar already so it wasn't like he was purposely checking for any females. However, Cartier had never seen the chick at the bar before.

"Hell, I don't know who that is," Cartier said before taking a sip from his Hennessey. "I ain't never seen that bitch though."

"Well, shit...I don't know 'bout you, but I'm 'bout to blow down on that ass," Stevie said confidently.

Cartier quickly intervened. "Nah, Stevie...you ain't got the proper *tools* to handle a bitch like that," he teased eyeing Starr's thick backside.

Stevie grinned inwardly. Starr was playing her role well, and Cartier's dumb ass was falling for the bait. He was far too cocky and obnoxious to let Stevie show him up. And he was too greedy to pass up on some new pussy even though he already had a girl and a baby at home.

"Oh, you finna holla at her?" Stevie asked. Her tone challenged him. "Ha! I bet she don't even give ya ass the time of day, bruh," she instigated.

Cartier sucked his teeth. "Hold this for me," he said handing Stevie his shot glass. "Watch and learn lil' nigga," he told her before swaggering off in Starr's direction.

Stevie scoffed. "Nah, nigga," she mumbled under her breath. "You watch...you just watch and wait," she said heading towards the exit.

Once outside, she walked hastily towards her vehicle. After climbing inside, she pulled on a black ski mask and waited patiently. Knowing her girl Starr, she could put the charm on a nigga quick. Hell, they had been sticking dudes up together for years.

Stevie finally watched the fish take the bait as Cartier followed Starr out of the bar. He looked like a horny ass dog ready to get his dick wet. Unfortunately, he had no idea what was in store for him.

Stevie watched as Starr climbed into the passenger side of Cartier's car. She grabbed the 9mm that lay on the passenger seat and slowly opened the driver's door.

***

Stevie released the smoke through slightly parted lips. She would have to play her cards right and have her best poker face on when she stepped to Rich.

If he found out that Stevie had anything to do with his brother's death, there was no telling what the hell he would do to her. That was main reason why Stevie wanted to make sure that Starr kept her mouth closed.

9

Starr was so engrossed in the news story being broadcast on the radio behind the counter of the gas station that she didn't even realize she was holding the line up. As expected, they were talking about Cartier's murder. Starr was listening out for any possible leads they might have.

"Your total is $4.16," the Arabic clerk said after ringing up everything Starr had put on the counter. A 20 oz. of Pepsi, pack of Starbursts, and a bag of Sun Chips. She had already pumped the gas using her debit card outside.

Starr didn't move in the slightest to retrieve her card to pay for the snacks.

"Excuse me, ma'am," the clerk called out. "$4.16 is your total," he repeated.

A sudden flashback of the flames coming off Cartier's car came to Starr's mind. She then reflected to the brutal way Stevie jammed her finger inside her wound last night. There was no way in hell she could tell anyone about the murder...not even her girl Diamond.

"I got it," a deep, sexy voice spoke up.

Starr finally snapped back to reality after realizing the guy behind her had just slapped a crisp fifty-dollar bill on the counter.

"Oh...uh—I got it," she spoke up. "I'm sorry," she apologized reaching in her purse. It was too late though. By the time she pulled out her wallet, the clerk was already handing the man behind her his change.

"Thank you," Starr said barely looking at the man. "I could've paid for it myself though." With that said she headed out of the gas station before the guy could even say 'you're welcome.'

Starr made her way towards her 2010 Hyundai Elantra. The man from the store was hot on her heels.

"Hey!" he called out. "Hey, hold up a second!"

Starr whirled around. "Look, I don't have any..." her voice trailed off as she got a good look at the guy calling out to her. He was fine as hell!

Antoine Jackson was six feet four inches tall, dark brown-skinned and rather slim in frame, but cut up from a daily workout regimen. A thin mustache and peach fuzz surrounded his full lips, and a pair of deep dimples rested in the center of his cheek. His somewhat slanted eyes were complemented by long dark eyelashes that curled slightly.

Antoine was sexy as hell in a pretty boy sort of way, but Starr was digging the sporty attire he wore which consisted of a fitted Nike t-shirt, a pair of basketball shorts, and the latest pair of Jordans on his feet.

I like pussy, Starr chastised herself. She had known for the better part of her life that she was into females. *So why the hell am I eyeing this nigga so hard?*

"I don't have any cash on me to pay you back," Starr told him assuming that's what he wanted.

Antoine chuckled. "Girl, I ain't thinkin' bout that lil' change," he told her. He extended his hand. "My name's Antoine and I was wonderin' if I could get your name...and possibly your number," he added.

"Sorry...no can do," Starr said heading towards her car.

Antoine didn't let up easily. "I mean what's up?" he asked. "You in a rush? You taken? Tell me somethin'."

Starr turned back around to face Antoine. "Both," she smiled.

"Well damn..." Antoine's dimples appeared as he grinned. "Can I at least get ya name, ma?" he asked.

Starr released a breath. Her lips thinned as she looked intensely at Antoine. "Starr," she finally said.

"Well, look," Antoine began. "Can I at least give you my number, Starr?" he asked. "In case ya nigga ever act up or you get curious about me?" he grinned.

Starr walked up towards her driver's door and opened it. Good thing Stevie wasn't with her right then. She would flip the fuck out if she saw someone hitting on Starr, *especially* a man. Stevie was beyond jealous when it came to her lady.

"You trying to get me in trouble?" Starr asked flirtatiously.

Antoine slowly made his way closer to Starr. "Nah, never that," he laughed. "I just see a beautiful woman, and I would hate to pass up the opportunity of gettin' to know you by not sayin' *somethin'*," he explained. "But I can dig that you in a relationship...however, if the situation does change—which I'm hoping it does," he joked, "I would love for you to hit me up. I'm a good dude."

Starr looked down. She suddenly found herself blushing and smiling. Antoine was just too cute. "You're a good dude, huh?" she asked.

"Fasho," he told her. "I'm single, I ain't got no kids. I gotta good head on my shoulders. I'm in school right now."

"Oh yeah?" Starr asked. Her interest was suddenly peaked. "What school you go to?"

"Cleveland State," he answered. "I play college ball. I also major in business and communication."

Oh he was communicating alright. He had Starr all ears by then. *What the hell are you doing girl*, she asked herself. *Just go ahead and take his number*, a part of her said.

"That's what's up," Starr nodded her head in approval.

"Well, look I ain't tryin' to hold you up Miss Lady," Antoine said. "Is it cool if I shoot you my number? No pressure to call," he smiled revealing those dimples. He knew they were his best feature as well as a woman's weakness.

Starr shrugged and pulled out her cell phone. She tried to play it cool. "Go for it."

Antoine rattled off his digits, and Starr plugged them into her cell phone under the name Ashley. There was no way in hell she would store his name under Antoine with the way Stevie stayed in her shit.

"Aight then," Starr said climbing into her car.

Antoine watched as she pulled off in her Elantra. Taken or not, he was certain she would hit him up sooner or later.

10

"What's up girl?" Starr greeted as she traipsed into the waiting area of Dillards.

"What's up?!" Diamond repeated in sarcasm." Bitch what took yo' ass so long? Had me out here waiting twenty damn minutes."

"I got held up at the damn gas station," Starr explained.

Together they made their way through the department store and towards the main entrance of Beachwood Mall.

Starr looked fly as hell in a red one sleeve crop top and a pair of tight black leather shorts. On her feet was a pair of cheetah print wedge booties. Diamond looked equally as bad in a white mesh skater dress and a pair of Red Bottoms. Every week they shared a little girl time and did some shopping together as if it were a ritual. It afforded them the leisure to just escape from the drama of their lives.

"How'd you end up getting held up at the gas station?" Diamond asked. She could be so nosey sometimes although unintentional.

Starr shrugged. "Some guy trying to talk to me," she said nonchalantly. She made it seem like it wasn't really a big deal.

Diamond snickered. "And what'd you do?" she asked. "Tell him that you prefer Tilapia over hot dogs?"

"I gave him my number," Starr admitted in a carefree tone.

Diamond instantly stopped in her tracks. She had to be sure that she heard her girl correctly. "You…Starr…gave your number to a man?" she asked. "Must be somebody you and Stevie trying to set up, huh?" she asked, her nosiness getting the best of her.

"Nah," Starr said. "It's nothin' like that. He seemed like a cool guy…"

Diamond's arched eyebrows raised in skepticism. "Cool guy?" She suddenly walked over to Starr and pressed the back of her hand against her forehead. "You feelin' aight? You must be drunk off Stevie's pussy juices or something," Diamond teased.

Starr playfully slapped Diamond's hand away. "He was cute, aight?" she finally admitted.

They continued walking towards the entrance of the mall.

Diamond shook her head. "I can't believe my girl Starr is finally crossing over to the other side," she teased. "'Bout damn time," she said. "I mean honestly. I never really understood what you saw in Stevie, you know? I mean, sure she looks like a dude, but what's the point in having a bitch that looks like a nigga when you could just have a nigga, you feel me?"

Starr shrugged. "You don't understand," she said in a soft tone.

"You're right," Diamond agreed. "I don't...so in that case enlighten me."

Starr released a deep sigh. "Stevie...we got history, you know? She knows me...I know her...I trust her," she added. "And it ain't too many mothafuckas I trust. She's just...," she paused. "She's there for me..."

"And a man can't be?" Diamond asked.

"Men are dogs," Starr interjected.

Diamond raised an eyebrow. "And Stevie isn't?" she asked.

"Stevie's got her moments," Starr said. "But she's like my comfort zone. I know what I'm getting with her."

Diamond frowned inwardly. Starr didn't *know* that damn much seeing as she didn't know her beloved Stevie had her head between Diamond's thighs on more than one occasion.

Starr continued. "It's like if I ventured outside of my comfort zone I wouldn't know what I was getting myself into with these niggas out here."

"But Starr you can't lie and tell me you don't miss the dick?" Diamond said. "And I'm not talking about no plastic shit Stevie be sticking up in ya ass, I'm talkin' some thick, hard, vein pulsatin' dick poundin' into that pussy!"

Starr laughed hysterically at her best friend's unfiltered language. A few customers turned and scowled in their direction, but neither woman gave a fuck.

"I mean...I *do* think about it from time to time," Starr admitted. "But that's all it is...thoughts, you know? I'm with Stevie...I love her..."

Diamond gave Starr a playful shove. "You don't love her that damn much. You saved that nigga's number in yo' phone!"

Starr broke into laughter after that remark.

"So you ever gon' call ole boy?" Diamond asked. "He must be really sexy if he got yo' dyke ass to give him the time of day," she teased.

Starr encased the tip of her tongue in her teeth. "Um...I don't know..." she smiled.

"You only live once Starr," Diamond said. "You only live once..."

Suddenly, Starr felt compelled to tell Diamond about the murder her and Stevie had committed. It had been on her mind lately and she needed someone to confide in.

"Diamond," she began. "I have to tell you something..."

Diamond turned to face Starr. "Alright...tell me," she said sarcastically.

Starr stopped in her tracks, grabbed Diamond by her wrist and led her towards a secluded area near the pants section of the department store.

"Look, when I tell you this, you gotta promise that you won't say shit about it to anyone, aight?" Starr asked. "You gotta take this shit to ya grave."

Diamond looked offended. "Hell, Starr I can hold water," she said.

Starr gave Diamond a knowing look. She had known Diamond long enough to know that her girl wasn't the best when it came to keeping secrets.

"Look, I promise, I won't say shit," Diamond swore.

Starr held out her pinky finger. "Pinky swear?" she asked.

Diamond rolled her eyes and sucked her teeth. "Oh my goodness, you so fuckin' childish," she laughed. "Pinky swear, aight? Now tell me the shit already."

Starr drew in a deep breath and released it. "Stevie and I," she began. "We killed a man," she finally blurted out.

Diamond was confused initially. "What?" she asked. "What do you mean ya'll killed a man?" she asked perplexed.

"Bitch, we bodied a nigga," Starr said sarcastically. "We killed him. Some nigga named Cartier."

Diamond's eyes widened. "You fuckin' serious?" she asked.

"It started out as just a stick up," Starr admitted. "But then shit got messy, he ended up jumping on Stevie," she said. "I stabbed dude in his back, and Stevie beat the shit out of his ass with a brick."

"How do you know you killed him?" Diamond asked with a serious expression.

"Trust me," Starr said. "He was dead...and if that brick ain't do the trick us throwin' his ass in the trunk of his car and setting it on fire sure did."

"Got damn, Starr," Diamond said in disbelief. "Ya'll was on some Ted Bundy type shit weren't ya'll?"

"You gotta promise you won't tell anybody about this shit," Starr said. "I mean it, Diamond. Nobody."

Diamond sighed deeply. "Aight," she agreed. "I won't tell a soul."

"And if you can," Starr added. "Just pretend that you didn't even hear this story," she said. "Stevie would flip if she knew I told you."

"I forgot about it already," Diamond said.

"Seriously, Diamond," Starr stressed.

Diamond placed her hand on Starr's shoulder and stared into her eyes. "Starr, you're my best friend...I swear I won't tell a soul. Trust me..."

***

A week later, Stevie made her way inside of Harvard Wine and Grille, a small bar located in the hood. Her nerves were understandably on edge since she was on her way to meet Rich.

It was the first time she had seen him since before Cartier had died. She didn't know what to expect.

She had no idea how and if she would be able to look this man in the eyes knowing she had killed his brother. Still Stevie held no remorse in her heart whatsoever. Cartier was a greedy, selfish egotistical son of a bitch who deserved everything he got.

Stevie heard that Cartier had to have a closed casket funeral, and she thought that shit was hilarious. As fucked up as it may have seemed she was actually proud of what she had done. The nigga Cartier was always dipping his fingers into her pay, and it was only right for her to do what she had to do.

However, Stevie wondered what exactly Rich had to say to her. He orchestrated the entire gun operation, and Stevie and Cartier were mere "street employees", handling the business and exchanges he was too busy to do. With Cartier out of the picture Stevie wondered if Rich would have some new blood running the operation with her. She hoped not. But she never knew when it came to Rich.

Coolio's *"Gangster's Paradise"* was playing on the Juke Box and the live band was still prepping for their performance.

Stevie found Rich at the bar sipping on a Corona. He was still wearing the suit from his brother's funeral earlier, and he looked out of it. For a brief second, Stevie actually felt remorseful, but she quickly pulled herself together and put on her best poker face.

She tapped Rich on the back. He slowly turned around and held his hand out. Stevie dapped him up, and Rich held up his hand for the bartender signaling for her to bring Stevie a beverage.

Rich ate and drank for free pretty much anywhere he went. He had earned mad love and respect from the streets.

"What's up, Rich boy," Stevie greeted taking a seat beside him. "I'm sorry to hear about the shit that happened to Cartier. That's some fucked up shit man." She prayed he wouldn't ask her why she didn't show up to the funeral. Hopefully, he didn't notice her absence and get suspicious.

Rich sighed and took a swig of his beer. "Yeah...well...that's the shit I wanted to holla at you about."

Stevie's heart sank to the pit of her stomach. *Did Rich know something,* she wondered.

"With Cartier gone, I'ma need you to run shit on ya own," he told her. "I ain't trustin' nobody else to handle my shit, and you already hold it down for me," he said. "You think you can handle the extra responsibility?" he asked. "I'll pay you three times as much as I did before."

If Stevie was any good at gymnastics she would have done a backflip right then and there in the bar. If she would have known what she knew now she would have bodied Cartier's ass a long time ago.

"Yeah, you know I gotchu'," Stevie told him.

Rich nodded his head in approval and dapped her up again. "You my lil' nigga," he told her. "Just know if you take care of me, I'll take care of you...You know how I am with mines."

"Fasho," Stevie nodded her head. "Fasho."

11

The sun was just beginning to set when Diamond made her way towards the entrance of the liquor store.

"Damn, what's up, ma! You got a man?"

As always, 'the thirsties'—as Diamond often referred to them—were standing around the outside of the liquor store in the Lee and Harvard Plaza. Their sole purpose was only to stand around and wait for any pretty lady to walk past so that they could hound her to death.

Diamond pointed to her BMW 5 series. Starr sat in the passenger side and was fixing her hair in the mirror. "You see that car," she asked. "If you ain't drivin' nothin' better than that don't even waste your breath tryin' to holla at me."

That comment immediately shut them down. With that said, Diamond sashayed inside the liquor store.

"Fuck that bougie ass hoe," one of the guys mumbled under his breath. Rejection never felt good.

As soon as Diamond entered the liquor store all eyes were on her. Even the Arabic cashiers were damn near drooling.

Diamond walked over towards the beverage cooler and retrieved a bottle of off brand apple juice. She then moseyed up to the counter. "Let me get a fifth of Hen."

"Aye...don't I know you, ma?" A deep, familiar voice spoke up.

Diamond turned around and prepared to tell off whoever had enough courage to approach her—however, she quickly stopped herself the moment she realized who it was.

Rich stood less than three feet from her wearing a black suit and egg white dress shirt underneath. The tie around his neck had been loosened, and his glassy eyes indicated that he was either drunk or high.

"You don't know me," Diamond corrected him. "But you've seen me around." She then turned towards the counter. "Let me get a bottle Hen," she told the cashier.

Rich walked up to Diamond. "Fantasy's," he said. "I told you you didn't make the cut..."

Diamond didn't look at him when she said, "You also told me you would call me." She then regretted saying that the moment it left her mouth. She didn't want this nigga thinking he had her feeling bitter or some shit.

"My fault, ma," Rich apologized. "I just buried my mufuckin' little brother, Cartier today," he admitted in a low tone.

Diamond finally turned around to face Rich. She didn't know why that name sounded so familiar.

Rich looked pained and disappointed. A complete opposite of the cocky way he had portrayed himself when they first met.

"I'm really sorry to hear that," she told him in a sincere voice.

"Hey," he said. "Shit happens. I'll be straight. The inevitable part of life is problems," he told her.

The cashier suddenly interrupted them after telling Diamond what her total was.

"I got it," Rich spoke up before placing a crisp hundred-dollar bill on the counter.

"Thank you," Diamond said.

The cashier bagged up the beverages and handed them to Rich. He obviously assumed Rich was her man, little did he know.

Rich followed Diamond out of the store. "Where you parked at ma?" he asked.

"Damn, Rich. That's you?" one of the guy's standing outside of the liquor store asked. As a matter of fact, he was the same guy that was trying to blow down on Diamond only moments earlier.

Rich turned to face the group of guys hanging around outside the liquor store. "Yo, don't worry about who the fuck this is," he spat. "Stop hangin' around the mufuckin' store, make yaself useful, and go make some damn money!" he barked.

The group of guys sighed, and rolled their eyes, and hesitantly did as they were told as they all walked off. Rich was that nigga.

Diamond pointed towards her BMW. "I'm right here," she told him.

"I see you ma," he smiled walking her towards her car.

Diamond opened the back seat and Rich carefully placed the drinks in the back. Oddly enough, he had no idea that one of his brother's murderers sat silently in the passenger seat of Diamond's car. They had no idea that they were somehow connected to each other.

Rich then closed the door and turned to face Diamond. She looked just as good as she did as the day they had met.

"Gimme some time to get my head together," he told her. "And then I'ma blow down on ya ass tough 'cause you know I'm feelin' you. You know that."

"I hear you," Diamond's lips pulled into a smirk.

"I want you. Real shit," Rich said before opening the driver's door.

Diamond climbed in and fastened her seat belt.

Rich politely closed the door behind her and tapped the hood. Diamond slowly navigated the car out of the parking spot and pulled off. He eyed her license plate which read: *Diamond.* She may have been driving a BMW 5 series, but fucking with a nigga like him, he could put her ass in a Bugatti, no problem.

***

"Aight, bitch you ready for this Apple Hen?!" Diamond yelled excitedly.

The two of them were at Starr's crib preparing to get geeked and talk shit like they did on most weekends. Usually by the time they established a good enough buzz, they would hit the club scene.

"You know it," Starr answered. She propped her bare feet on top of the coffee table.

Diamond poured and mixed their beverages on the kitchen island.

"So," Starr began. "Who was ole buddy back at the liquor store?" she asked. "I see ya ass been withholding info from me. I thought we were better than that bitch."

"Oh, girl he's just some dude I met at the strip club," Diamond answered nonchalantly.

"Which one?" Starr asked. "And why you ain't invite me? Maybe I wanted to see some ass and titties bounce," she joked.

"Girl, I was trying to see if I could make some extra money at Fantasy's. But he told me I wasn't good enough to work there."

"Fantasy's?!" Diamond blurted. "Hol' up! Hol' up! Hol' the fuck up! That was Rich Keys?!" she asked excitedly. "*THEE* Rich Keys?!"

Diamond walked over towards the sofa Starr sat on and joined her. She then handed Starr her glass. "Damn, bitch you saying his name like he's a celebrity or some shit."

"Hoe, he *is* a celebrity damn near," Starr corrected her friend. "You don't even know who the hell he really is!"

"Bitch, you didn't even know who he was either til' I just told you," Diamond laughed before taking a sip of her drink.

"Oh, I know about Mr. Rick Keys, *beeleedat*," Starr giggled.

"Well then tell me something, hoe," Diamond said.

"Rich Keys was like one of the biggest drug lords in Cleveland's history," Starr explained. "Hell a lot of these niggas wouldn't even be out here doing what they were doing if it weren't for Rich. He was that nigga in the 90s and early 2000s. I heard that he ended up doing a bid, and ever since he's been out he's been on the straight and narrow or some shit. Legit. But," she added. "In my opinion, I think he's moving weight out of those clubs and bars he owns. Once a hustler always a hustler," she said. "The nigga's just smarter now."

Diamond absorbed Starr's words and allowed them to sink in.

"Ole Diamond got herself a hood celebrity," Starr teased. "But on the real though...be careful with a nigga like him Di."

12

"Do you want me to—"

"Ssshh. Ssshh," Rich quickly cut off Tatiana before she could finish her sentence. He wasn't in the mood to hear anything she had to say to be honest.

Rich had called her over, because he needed someone to release his pent-up frustration inside of plain and simple. Tatiana was a dancer at his strip club, Fantasy's and he kept her around for intimate purposes only.

Tatiana pulled off her jacket and hung it over the barstool in the kitchen.

Rich poured the both of them a shot of 151 Bacardi. He needed some strong shit that was capable of numbing the pain he didn't feel like dealing with.

He handed Tatiana her shot glass and together they tossed back the liquor.

"*Eehhhh*," Rich hissed as the liquor burned his throat. He then motioned for Tatiana to come closer. "Come here," he said.

Tatiana slowly made her way towards Rich. She was a sexy ass woman that reminded him of a brown-skinned Nia Long with the same haircut and all.

"Promise me something," he said staring into her dark eyes.

Tatiana stared earnestly into Rich's glazed over eyes. She could tell he was tipsy, but she wasn't surprised. Hell, he had just buried his brother today.

"Yes. Anything," she said eagerly.

Tatiana as well as several other chicks in Fantasy's had been fighting—oftentimes literally—for the wifey position, but none had quite earned the label. Little did they know, Rich had no intentions whatsoever of 'wifing' of a fucking stripper, however he'd dig their backs out all night long.

"Promise me something," Rich continued. "Promise me you won't say another mufuckin' word from now til' the time you leave," he said. "Can you promise me that?"

Tatiana's nodded her head. She wasn't expecting for him to say that.

"Thank you," Rich slurred clearly intoxicated. "The least I deserve is no damn conversation. Hell, I gotta lot of shit on my mind." With that said he walked over towards the kitchen island and snorted the thin line of coke he had carefully laid out.

After snorting a fair portion up both his nostrils, he took Tatiana by the hand and led her towards his bedroom.

Just to be in Rich's house was a privilege. He owned a luxurious eight-bedroom, eleven bathroom mini mansion in Shaker Heights, Ohio.

Once inside Rich's bedroom Tatiana immediately began to undress. Rich unbuttoned his dress shirt and stepped out of his slacks.

Tatiana already knew what time it was as she climbed into Rich's four poster California king size bed and tooted her ass up in the air.

Rich retrieved a Magnum from the drawer, and climbed into the bed. The mattress creaked beneath his weight. After rolling the magnum down his dick he slid inside Tatiana's tight, wet pussy.

"*Mmm*," she whimpered.

Rich wet his thumb and then slowly slid it inside Tatiana's asshole. With his free hand, he squeezed on her soft, round ass cheek.

"Throw it back," he told her. "You know how daddy like that shit."

Tatiana's cheeks flushed as she fought to keep up with Rich's harsh strokes. He was taking all his frustrations out on Tatiana's pussy.

"Not so hard baby," she moaned.

"What did I tell you?" Rich asked. "I told you not to say shit else, didn't I?" He gave her left ass cheek a firm slap, and she yelped out in pain.

Tatiana dropped her face into the cotton pillow on the bed, as she muffled her screams. Rich was fucking the shit out of her unlike ever before.

He lifted his right leg up, and held onto Tatiana's waist as he stroked her from behind. His balls slapped against her swollen clit.

Her walls were gripping his thick dick as he pounded into her. "Damn...," he groaned. "I'm finna cum..."

Tatiana reached between her thighs and began stroking her wet clit.

Moments later, they came simultaneously.

Rich collapsed on the side of Tatiana. He then folded his hands behind his back and stared up at the tray ceiling of his bedroom.

Tatiana continued to respect his wishes of silence as she climbed out the bed and padded towards the master bathroom.

Life's a bitch and then you die, Rich thought to himself.

***

Stevie stumbled into her apartment drunk out of her mind after celebrating the great news. Starr and Diamond were chilling, drinking, and laughing on the sofa as they reminisced about the good old days. They were so caught up in their conversation that they had completely forgotten about their plans to go out.

However, they were both too drunk to drive anywhere. The effects of the liquor had the two women feeling nice.

Starr was the first to notice Stevie enter the house. "What's up babe," she greeted.

Stevie took one look at Diamond and frowned. The first thing that came to mind was that Starr had gotten comfortable enough to tell Diamond about the two of them killing Cartier.

Whenever Stevie had a little liquor in her system, she began acting paranoid, and out of character. She also got unreasonably angry— oftentimes for no damn reason.

"Where you comin' from bay?" Starr asked.

"Celebrating," Stevie slurred. Her eyes never left Diamond. "What the fuck ya'll in here talking and giggling about?" she asked in a nasty tone.

Diamond sucked her teeth. "None of your damn business, Stevie. Damn."

Diamond was just fucking around with Stevie, but Stevie automatically took it personally. She was always twice as sensitive when she had been drinking.

"Bitch, what?" Stevie snapped. "Hoe, I'm not even talkin' to you! I'm talkin' to my fuckin' girl." Her gaze then wandered over towards Starr who had a surprised expression on her face. "Like I said, what the fuck ya'll talkin' and laughin' about?"

Diamond waved her hand in a dismissive tone. "Stevie, bye," she said. "You obviously drunk."

Stevie immediately flipped the hell out. "Bitch, you know what?! Get up and get the fuck out my house!" she spat.

Diamond looked taken back and offended. "What?" Initially she didn't take Stevie seriously. Never had she literally kicked Diamond out her house.

"You heard me!" Stevie yelled. "Get your mothafuckin' ass up and get out."

When Diamond didn't move quick enough, Stevie charged over towards Diamond, roughly snatched her out her seat and forced her towards the front door.

"Stevie, what the fuck are you doing?!" Diamond yelled. "Get your fucking hands off me!

You trippin'!" She tried to shake Stevie off and pull away from her, but Stevie was much stronger by far.

Stevie swung the front door open and shoved Diamond into the hallway.

"Bitch, you just gon' kick me out?! I'm drunk as fuck!" Diamond yelled. "I can't drive!"

"That ain't my fuckin' problem!" Stevie yelled before slamming the door in Diamond's face.

It wasn't until then that Diamond noticed she was barefoot. "Ain't this a bitch?" she asked herself.

13

"Stevie, what the fuck is up with you?" Starr asked in astonishment.

"Did you tell her any fucking thing?" Stevie asked walking over towards Starr.

"What the hell are you talking about?" Starr asked. "Tell her what?!"

WHAP!

Stevie slapped Starr upside her head. "Bitch, you know what the fuck I'm talkin' bout! Stop acting stupid!" she yelled.

Starr's hands flew up to block her face from the several blows that followed soon after. "What is your problem?!" she cried. "Stevie you're drunk! *Stop hitting me!*"

"Did you tell Diamond about the shit we did?!" Stevie asked. "Huh?!"

Tears streamed from Starr's eyes. "No I didn't!" she cried. "*I swear!*"

Stevie roughly grabbed Starr's face and yanked her head back to look in her eyes. "I'm not fucking around Starr! I told you not tell anyone shit!"

"I swear!" Starr cried.

Stevie finally released Starr's face, and relaxed. "My bad, bay...I was just—"

Starr quickly got up and tried to walk around Stevie. However, Stevie quickly grabbed her by the wrist, stopping Diamond in her tracks.

"Starr, I said I'm sorry."

Starr quickly snatched away from Stevie. "Sorry doesn't mean shit to me, Stevie," Starr said gritted teeth. "You said you were done with the bullshit, but it's obvious you ain't gon' ever change," she said. "I'm leaving you, Stevie. Straight up."

"What?!" Stevie yelled. "Fuck you mean you leavin' me?!"

"Just like you heard!" Starr lashed out. "I'm done with you and yo' shit. It's over—"

"Over?!" Stevie repeated in disbelief. "All the shit we done been through together, you just gon' say it's over?!" she asked. "So what you gon' do, Starr?! Huh?!" she yelled. "Run to one of these sorry ass niggas in the street that probably got all types of STDs and shit?! Is that what you want?! A man?!" Stevie looked enraged, but her tone was laced with disappointment.

"Maybe that's what I need!" Starr retorted.

Stevie looked as if Starr had just slapped her in the face. "Oh! That's what you want bitch?!" she yelled. "*Some dick*?!" Suddenly Stevie ran towards their bedroom, and re-emerged seconds later with an eight-inch black dildo.

"Here! This what you want, hoe?!" Stevie viciously grabbed Starr by her hair, and snatched her head back.

Without warning, she jammed the dildo deep inside Starr's mouth forcing her to suck and gag on the plastic toy.

Gagging and gurgling noises came from Starr's throat as she struggled to push Stevie off her. She could barely breathe as the toy blocked off her air supply.

Stevie jammed the toy further down Starr's throat. Her watery eyes rolled to the back of her head as she struggled to gasp for air. One more inch did the trick.

Starr suddenly spit up a mouthful of vomit. Stevie stepped away from her not wanting to get covered in throw up.

Starr helplessly dropped onto her hands and knees, coughing and spitting up vomit while greedily sucking in air.

Stevie laughed sadistically. "Bitch, you wanted the dick, but look like you can't even handle it."

Starr wiped away the saliva from her mouth, and slowly stood to her feet. Stevie folded her arms across her chest, and shook her head feeling like she had proved her point.

Suddenly, Starr walked over to Stevie and punched her dead in the mouth!

Stevie's head snapped back from the impact of the blow. She quickly reached up and grabbed her mouth. "You fucking bitch!" she cried.

Starr grabbed her purse and car keys off the kitchen island, and headed out of the apartment ignoring Stevie's curses and threats.

***

Diamond squinted her eyes and leaned up in her seat as she fought to focus on the road. She had just hopped onto 90 West...bad idea.

"I should've taken the fuckin' streets," she cursed herself. Diamond swerved in and out of lanes as she prepared to come around the bin that merged with the four-lane freeway.

Suddenly, Diamond's cell phone vibrated in the passenger seat. It was her girl Starr calling to let her know everything that had just happened.

Driving over forty miles an hour, Diamond swerved a little as she reached over taking her eyes off the road briefly. She lifted the phone up to survey the caller ID—

Her car suddenly swerved towards the shoulder of the road before slamming grill first into the highway median!

Everything seemingly happened in slow motion. The hood of Diamond's BMW caved inward after the forceful impact. Without a seatbelt fastened across her chest, her body quickly lunged forward, sailing through the windshield. The weight of her body shattered the glass.

Diamond's body flew through the shattered windshield like a ragdoll! Her left leg painfully collided with the concrete median, snapping her bone in two. Diamond landed on her right arm the wrong way shattering the bone to pieces. She was unconscious before she even hit the ground.

14

Starr hung her cell phone up once it finally brought her to Diamond's voicemail. She figured her girl was probably still upset about the way Stevie had up and kicked her out.

Starr cruised towards the east side of Cleveland. She honestly didn't have a destination in mind, but just needed the space from Stevie. She couldn't believe what she had just done, and most of all Starr couldn't believe she had gathered up enough courage to hit Stevie. Never in their four-year relationship had Starr had ever hit Stevie no matter how often Stevie put her hands on her.

Starr wasn't a fighter. She never had been. But the shit Stevie had just pulled called for more than just a sock in the mouth. Starr pulled out her cell phone again, and called Diamond. Once again, she was sent to her voicemail.

"Damn," Starr cursed to herself. She was actually looking forward to spending the night over Diamond's house just to get away from Stevie. "Where is this chick?" she asked herself.

***

An ambulance, fire truck, and several police cars surrounded the car accident that had occurred less than a half hour ago. Two lanes were closed off and a traffic jam had quickly occurred.

Diamond's fragile body was hoisted into an ambulance on a stretcher, and she was immediately rushed to St. Vincent's Hospital.

***

Rich tossed a stack of singles onto Tatiana aka Luxury as she did her thing on the stage of Fantasy's Gentlemen Club. It was sort of like a ritual to get the fellas hype enough to throw money too.

Some niggas didn't mind spending paper, but there were others who had to be somewhat coaxed.

Short hair like Nia Long...

Loose ones she don't need a loan...

Start twerkin' when she hear her song...

Stripper pole her income...

Rich took a swig from his beer and tossed the remainder of singles at Tatiana's pedicured feet.

Heading back to the bar, he took a seat on the stool. Rich had finally changed out of the suit into his regular street attire. He started not to even come to his own strip club tonight, but he still had a business to run and money to make.

After blowing Tatiana's back out they both made their way to the strip club. Tatiana, to make her income, and Rich to oversee the club. Being a boss wasn't easy.

The bartender Sasha slid an ice-cold Corona in front of him, and popped the cap off. Rich didn't even ask for the beverage. She just knew how Rich got down.

Everyone that evening pretty much kept their distance from Rich. Because of the loss of his brother, they understood and respected his nerves were on edge, and no one wanted to become a victim of his aggression.

The bartender sauntered off.

Rich continued to sip on his beer as he stared at one of the many flat screen TVs in the club. The eleven o'clock 19 Action News was on and they were talking about and showing footage of a car accident that had just taken place on 90 east.

Rich squinted his eyes to get a good look at the smashed-up vehicle on the television screen. He knew he wasn't tripping when he noticed the make and model of the car, and more importantly the license plate that read: *Diamond*.

15

Two Weeks Later

Diamond had been placed in a medically induced coma subsequently to the car crash in order to protect her brain from swelling. A fractured collar bone, broken arm, and broken leg had been the consequence of drinking and driving. Not to mention, Diamond having to pay for city damages. Things could have been much worse though. She could have died.

While in the medically induced coma, Diamond was in a paralyzed-like state. She could hear everything around her, including conversation, but she could not move or speak.

Diamond had heard Stevie and Starr visit her on countless occasions. She had even felt Stevie's soft lips against hers while Starr took a quick bathroom break. Stevie had even apologized about her actions the night she had kicked Diamond out.

Diamond's mother had only visited her once. Diamond knew without a doubt it was her mom, because she could always smell the scent of booze on her breath mingled with cheap perfume.

Diamond and her mother had never gotten along. It seemed as if the moment Barbara

Ann Baker had pushed Diamond out of her pussy, they seemingly hated one another. Barbara was a neglectful alcoholic and Diamond resented her mother for never being there for her. Barbara despised Diamond just because of the way she lived her life. None of their family liked or respected Diamond simply because her own mother had disowned her.

"Look at you," Barbara whispered in her raspy voice one afternoon. Leaning towards Diamond, she stared down at her sleeping daughter in disgust. "Laying up in this got damn hospital looking crazy." Barbara sucked her yellow tinted teeth and shook her head. She looked three times her actual age due to alcohol abuse and a harsh life. "You should have done this world a damn favor and just died...you hear me little bitch...you should've just died."

Diamond may have not been able to respond, but she felt the pain from her mother's hurtful words.

"I oughta pull the plug on your ass right now—"

"If you touch her, you gon' have a fuckin' serious problem with me," a calm familiar deep voice said.

Diamond listened intently as someone suddenly entered her hospital room.

There was silence from Barbara for a brief moment before she asked, "Who the hell are you?"

Rich didn't miss a beat. "I'ma be the last mufucka you will ever see if you touch that damn plug," he told her. "As a matter of fact, gon' get the fuck outta here and don't bring yo' sorry ass back," he spat.

Barbara scowled at Rich, but didn't utter another word. In her day and age, she was totally unable to defend herself, especially from a nigga like Rich. Without another word, she quickly left the room.

Rich slowly walked over towards Diamond's bed, looked down at her, and carefully moved a few strands of hair from her face.

The cuts and bruises on her face had finally healed, and aside from the cast on her leg and arm she was looking healthier by the day.

Unbeknownst to Diamond, Rich was covering her medical expenses as well as the damages she had caused to city property. He was still trying to figure out why he was even helping this chick out. He didn't know her personally, he had only run into her twice, and he had never even hit. However, there was something about her.

Rich couldn't figure out what exactly that something was...but whatever it was had propelled him to rush to the hospital the moment he saw the news. The entire situation really fucked him up because he had just seen her hours before the accident even took place.

Diamond's eyelids twitched a little upon his gentle touch, but she didn't open her eyes. Rich lowered his hand, and slowly made his way towards the door.

***

The following afternoon Starr grabbed a bouquet of artificial orchids, and placed them inside her shopping basket. She needed a few little knick knacks from the store, and decided to grab some flowers on the way to see Diamond.

Starr still couldn't believe the shit that had happened to her girl. It seemed like just yesterday, they were kicking it, shopping, drinking, and just loving life. Things didn't start to go downhill until Stevie stormed into the house and tossed Diamond out.

Starr sighed. Speaking of Stevie, she had taken her no-good ass back...as always. With Diamond in the hospital, Starr felt like she needed Stevie now more than ever as a support system.

Diamond and Starr had been friends for so long that Diamond was more so like an actual sister than a friend.

Starr made her way towards the twenty items or less line, but stopped in midstride to eye the cover of the Cosmopolitan magazine.

"Hey you," a familiar voice greeted.

Starr slowly turned around. Standing a few feet from where she stood was Antoine, the guy she had met at the gas station a couple weeks ago.

Instead of the sporty attire he wore the first time they had met, he was now rocking a pair of loose fitting True Religions, a black fitted V-neck t-shirt that hugged his firm, chiseled torso, and a pair of clean Timberland boots.

"Hey," Starr greeted less enthusiastic. Her gaze wandered towards his shopping cart. There were a few frozen dinners and bunch of snacks. Typical foods for a single man.

Antoine smiled. "This is our second time bumping into each other," he said. "It must be fate."

Starr shrugged. "Or must be that someone's following the other."

Antoine chuckled. "Well, I'm flattered," he teased.

Starr couldn't help but to smile and shake her head at Antoine's sense of humor. "So," she said. "That's what you think? I've been following you?" she laughed.

Antoine admired the cute little gap between her front teeth. "I tend to have that effect on women," he joked. "I would much rather you just call me though."

Starr hesitated. "Wish it was that easy..."

"What's so hard about picking up a phone and dialing seven numbers?" he laughed.

Starr shifted her weight to one leg and stared at Antoine in awe. She admired his deep dimples. He was so cute to her. She opened her mouth to say something but closed it when she realized she didn't know exactly what to say.

"What are you about to do right now?" Antoine asked. "I've got two and a half hours until my next class. How about we grab a bite to eat together?"

Starr sighed and hesitated briefly. "I— uh...I don't know—"

"Starr, it's just lunch," he told her with a charming smile. "I'm not asking for your hand in marriage."

Starr mulled it over...

16

Twenty minutes later, Starr and Antoine sat across from each other in a booth inside of The Corner Alley in downtown Cleveland. The place doubled as a bowling alley and trendy restaurant.

Starr had never dined there before. As a matter of fact, she seldom dined out unless it was with Diamond. Stevie was so preoccupied with making cash that she rarely ever took Starr anywhere unless it was to plan to stick some random nigga up.

"I never been here before," Starr said looking around.

"Really?" Antoine asked. "This is a nice lil' spot. Me and the boys on the team usually hit this spot up on the weekends. It be jumpin'.'"

"So do you like it?" Starr asked.

"Like what?" Antoine asked clearly perplexed. "This restaurant?"

Starr giggled. "No," she answered. "It's obvious you like the restaurant or else you wouldn't have brought me here," she said smiling. "I meant do you like being in college? What's it like?" she asked obviously interested in the subject.

"I mean, it's straight," he shrugged. "Feels good to know I'm doing something other than running the streets. Somethin' positive."

Starr folded her hands and placed them under her chin. "I always thought I would go to college," she admitted. She had never told anyone else that. She figured Diamond and Stevie would laugh in her face.

Antoine stared earnestly at Starr. "And what happened?" he asked.

Starr snorted. "Life," she said flatly. "Life happened. Hell, I didn't even finish high school," she admitted. She wasn't ashamed by the facts. It was what it was.

"Well, you know it's never too late," he suggested. "It's plenty of programs that help people obtain their high school diplomas."

Starr chuckled and shook her head. "Me and school," she paused and thought about it. "Nah...I've already chosen my path in life," she said. "And it doesn't involve an education."

Antoine shrugged. "School's not for everyone."

Starr liked how nonchalant Antoine had said it. She also liked and appreciated that he didn't seem judgmental towards her like so many other people when she told them she dropped out of high school.

"So can I ask you something?"

"What's up?" Starr asked.

"Do you have any goals? Anything you wanna do with ya life?"

Starr carefully thought about her response. She then shook her head and smiled to herself.

Antoine grinned. "What?" he asked. "What you smiling about?"

Starr looked up at Antoine. She didn't know him from Adam, but he had this look in his eyes...a look of determination. A look of someone who rarely if ever gave up.

Starr immediately wondered what he saw in her eyes—if he saw anything. She wondered if he saw the lack of determination in her eyes. She wondered if he could see that she had given up on her hopes and dreams long ago.

"I...uh...I always used to say I wanted to be an actress," she told him. "It was just some silly thought I used to have as a kid."

Antoine stared intensely at Starr almost as if he were trying to read her. She could tell he was the type of person that broke down everything a person said and analyzed it. Starr began to feel slightly uncomfortable. She didn't want him trying to figure her out like she was a damn puzzle.

Starr quickly cleared her throat. "What about you?" she asked quickly turning the table. "I know you're in college and everything, but what do you really hope to gain from it?"

Antoine smiled. "I would like to get drafted to the NBA."

Starr raised an eyebrow. "Really?" She nodded her head in approval. "Any team you got in mind?"

"Shit...my hometown," Antoine beamed. "Cleveland."

Starr decided to challenge him. "You think you're good enough to get drafted?" she asked with a half smirk.

Antoine smiled. "I don't think I'm good enough," he told her. "I know I am."

Starr raised an eyebrow. "Someone's cocky."

"I'm not cocky," he explained. "I'm just good at what I do."

"For real?"

"Real talk...You should come see me play one day."

Before Starr could respond, their waitress finally returned with their lunch. Starr ordered a house Caesar salad and Antoine ordered a teriyaki burger.

As soon as Starr began to dig into her salad, her cell phone suddenly began to vibrate on the table. Both Antoine and Starr's gaze wandered towards the cell phone. Of course it was Stevie.

Starr started to just hit the ignore button but then decided to just turn the phone off completely.

17

Diamond's eyes slowly opened. Her vision was initially blurry as she stared at the several fuzzy faces looking down at her. The chemicals had finally been degraded by her body, and she was suddenly relieved from the coma.

Dizziness was the first thing Diamond felt, followed by confusion. "Where...where am I?" she asked in a hoarse tone.

"Ms. Baker, you've been in a medically induced coma for a little over two weeks. You were in a horrific car accident on the freeway that left both your right arm and left leg broken. There was also swelling around the brain as well as a minor contusion," her doctor explained.

"A car accident...?" she repeated in disbelief. Her vision was finally getting clearer.

Diamond tried to sit up in bed, but the effort was futile. She quickly noticed her broken leg was plastered and elevated in traction.

"Fuck," she cursed. How the hell was she going to pay her bills like this? There weren't any niggas in the world willing to pay for some handicap ass pussy.

The doctor noticed her irritation and offered some quick words of reassurance that meant little next to nothing to Diamond. Once he felt he had said all he needed to say he departed with one of the nurses by his side. One fair-skinned nurse stayed behind and fluffed Diamond's pillow for her.

"If you need anything please be sure to let me know," she smiled cheerfully.

Diamond wished she would stop smiling in her damn face. There wasn't a fucking thing worth smiling about. "My life is fucked," she told herself.

The nurse was just on her way out, but she turned on her heel the moment she heard Diamond speak. "What's that ma'am?" she asked politely.

Diamond sighed in frustration. "I said my life is fucked," she repeated. "I have no car, I'm sitting up here fucked up in the hospital, and I'm going to have to pay a shit load of money for the hospital bill," she complained. "Can my life get any worse?"

The nurse frowned and offered Diamond a look of sympathy. "You could be far less fortunate," she said. "You were actually one of the lucky ones," she smiled. "And you've got a great support system. I'm sure they'll be there for you."

Diamond scoffed. "Support system?" she laughed. "Who and what is that?" she asked in a sarcastic tone.

"Two females came to see you quite often," she said.

Diamond rolled her eyes at the very thought of Starr and Stevie. If it hadn't been for them and their bullshit she wouldn't even be in this mess.

"And there was also a man that came to see you almost every day. I take it he was your husband...fiancé?"

Diamond's eyebrows furrowed. "A man?" she asked confused.

Diamond was pretty sure none of her tricks knew about the accident yet, so she wondered what man the nurse was referring to.

"Just know you have people that care about you," the nurse said before leaving the room.

Two minutes after the nurse walked out, Starr suddenly walked in. She looked great in a leather jacket with silver spikes on the shoulders, acid wash jeggings, and black combat boots.

Diamond rolled her eyes out of jealousy. Here she was laying in a hospital bed with her leg and arm in a cast and Starr was unintentionally stunting on her.

"Don't be rolling your eyes at me, bitch," Starr said playfully. "I see you're awake." She made her way towards Diamond's bed. "I brought you some flowers." She placed them on the stand near the hospital bed.

"Fuck you and those fake ass flowers," Diamond said out of spite.

"You mad at me?" Starr asked. She sounded genuinely hurt.

Diamond childishly turned her head away from Starr.

Starr's mouth fell open in disbelief. "You really are mad at me," she said. "I didn't know Stevie was going to come home and flip like that, I swear. Believe me, Diamond, she feels awful about all this shit that happened to you. She feels like it's all her fault."

Diamond snorted and shook her head.

Starr leaned extremely close to Diamond's bed and moved her face near Diamond's. Once it was obvious that Diamond wouldn't make eye contact, Starr turned Diamond's chin towards her.

"Me and Stevie been coming almost every day to see ya ass. We're here for you," she said. "So please don't be mad, aight?"

Diamond didn't respond as she stared at her best friend.

Starr leaned closer and placed a quick, innocent kiss on Diamond's lips. She then released her face and took a seat beside the hospital bed. "We were even going to try to take care of the medical bills, but someone already beat us to the task," Starr said with a sneaky smile.

Diamond looked confused. "What do you mean someone already beat you to the task?" she asked.

Starr bit her bottom lip and grinned. "Well, friend," she said. "Word is you got that nigga, Rich paying your medical bills. He even came up here to see you a couple times."

"Rich?" Diamond asked confused.

"Rich Keys, bitch! You know who Rich is!" Starr joked. "Hoe you might have been in a coma, but ya ass ain't got amnesia," she teased.

"What do you mean Rich came up here?" Diamond asked. "Why would he do that?"

Starr opened her mouth, but her gaze suddenly wandered over towards the entrance of the room.

Standing in the doorway wearing a smug expression on his face was Richard Keys. He wore a black sweatshirt, a pair of camouflage trousers, and on his feet were a pair of Timberland boots. A 14 ct. gold watch set the outfit off. As always he was fitted, and dressed to impress.

He slowly made his way inside the hospital room. There was so much tension in the air that one could slice a knife through it. Both women's eyes were fastened to him.

Rich then looked from Diamond to Starr. She suddenly became apprehensive, cleared her throat, and stood to her feet. "Well...um...I'ma gon' head and get out of here...leave you two alone," she stammered. A smirk played in the corner of her lips. She already knew what time it was.

Diamond watched as Starr hurriedly left the hospital room. *Damn. Her punk ass didn't even say bye*, she said to herself.

Rich took a seat in the chair that Starr had previously been sitting in.

"I'm glad to see you're finally up," he said. His tone was very nonchalant, but the fact that he was even there let Diamond know that he cared.

Then again, why was he even there to begin with? "My girl told me you were taking care of my medical bills," Diamond didn't beat around the bush.

"Yes," Rich answered. "You got that."

Diamond was confused. "But why?" she asked. "Why you doing this for me? You don't even know me."

Rich chuckled and ran a hand over his silky brush waves. "Shit, I'm still tryin' to figure that out myself," he told her. "The only excuse I can think of is…hell, I like ya ass…"

"You like me?" Diamond repeated in disbelief. "You're doing this because you like me?"

Rich turned to face Diamond. His expression became serious. "Look, I ain't gon' beat around the bush," he told her. "I'ma very impulsive nigga. When I want something, I'll do any and everything in my power to get it."

His eyes roamed over Diamond's beautiful face. She looked weary. Her hair was disheveled, her lips were dry, and there were still a few semi-healed scratches and bruises on her face. However, she was still a bad bitch in his eyes. Rich knew Diamond's potential, and she was a gem, so seeing her now at her worse didn't mean shit to him.

"I want you," he stated.

Diamond's eyebrows rose. "You don't even know me," she said again.

Rich didn't miss a beat. "Shit, I can get to know you," he said.

"What are you going to do with my handicap ass," she laughed. "My fucking arm is broke...my leg's in a cast—"

"I'll take care of ya ass. I gotchu," he smiled.

Diamond stared at Rich in disbelief. "You're serious?" she asked.

"Dead serious."

Diamond looked confused. "But...why...why me? Why not one of the many chicks who strip at your club?"

"I don't want none of those hoes the way I want you," he said. "Like I told you in the club, pussy is pussy...that shit ain't hard for a nigga like me to obtain." Rich sat up in his seat. "Look, I don't know what type of niggas you used to fuckin' with, but recognize I ain't the average. The sooner you see that shit, the sooner you'll know you're fuckin' with a real nigga."

18

Starr sat in the parking lot of the hospital. Instead of going straight home she held her cell phone in her hand. She was fighting the temptation to do something she had no business even thinking about.

Suddenly, Starr had a flashback of Stevie slapping her, hitting her, and brutally shoving the dildo in her mouth.

Fuck her, Starr thought.

Without a second thought, she sent a text message to Antoine that said: *I really enjoyed myself with you earlier.*

Starr wasn't expecting a response from him so suddenly, but he did. She anxiously read his message: *What are you doing this evening?*

***

Later that evening Rich and Stevie sat side by side at the bar sipping on their beers. Most of the people there were engrossed in the NFL game.

"So I'm guessing she was everything I said she would be and more?" Stevie suddenly asked. She wasn't a fool and she knew that Rich was digging Diamond tough.

Rich turned to face Stevie and grinned. "You got that," he told her. "She's bad than a mufucka."

He then reached in his pocket and slid a small wad of cash to Stevie. The money wasn't related to the business operation she ran for him. Instead it was for leading Diamond right to him.

"And she's worth it," he added.

Stevie pocketed the cash. She knew exactly what she was doing when she suggested Diamond to check out Fantasy's Gentlemen's club. She knew Diamond's curiosity would eventually get the best of her, and besides she loved money. Diamond was bound to check out the spot. However, unbeknownst to her, Rich had been expecting her arrival sooner or later. He had some big plans for Diamond.

"I hope she is," Stevie said. "That chick can be a handful..."

***

"So how was your hospital visit?" Antoine asked Starr as they strolled through the park together.

The sun was just beginning to set, but the view was absolutely breathtaking especially since they were near Lake Erie.

"It was brief. Didn't last very long at all." Starr answered. "She ended up having another visitor a little after I first got there so I went ahead and dismissed myself."

Antoine nodded his head. "I can dig it," he said.

They continued to walk down a narrow path that was surrounded by an array of beautiful flowers and roses.

"So...um," Antoine began. "You happy with the person you're with?"

Starr sighed. For some reason she knew the question was going to come about sooner or later. "I'm content more than anything," she answered.

"Content and happiness are two different things," he said.

"I'm comfortable," Starr added.

"Comfort and happiness are two different things," he said.

Starr broke into a fit of laughter. "Um...it's complicated," she said. "That's all I can say."

Antoine shook his head. "Yo, I never understand ya'll women," he said.

Starr looked up at him. "What do you mean?" she asked.

Antoine shrugged. "I just don't see how ya'll can fuckin' settle," he said. "Especially when ya'll deserve the best."

19

Starr and Antoine were seated at the bar inside of the Chocolate Bar located in downtown Cleveland an hour after they had first met up. They were enjoying one another's company, laughing, and getting to know more about each other over drinks.

For a moment, Starr had actually allowed herself to push Stevie to the back of her mind. And honestly it felt good.

"So is college anything similar to high school?" Starr asked before taking a sip of her Margarita.

Antoine chuckled. "Nah...nothing like it, ma," he told her. "Hell, in high school the teachers held your hand...in college the professors could give two shits if you understand the material or not," he said. "Either you keep up or you get left behind."

"So I take it you do well?" Starr asked.

Antoine scoffed. "Finally after three semesters. Hell, my second year I landed my ass on Academic Probation, and the only reason I got my shit together was because the coach threatened to kick me off the team."

"I could never last in college," Starr admitted.

Antoine's expression turned serious. "Woman, why do you keep saying what you can't do?" he asked. "You will never know what you're capable of until you try it," he said. "I'ma need for you to start havin' a lil' bit more faith in yaself, ma."

Starr started to respond, but suddenly her cell phone vibrated indicating she had just received a text message. She pulled out her phone and scanned the text message. Of course it was from Stevie: *Bitch, where the fuck u at?? I been blowin ya ass up! I got a lick for us tonight! Call me ASAP!*

Starr sighed in frustration. Evidently Stevie had just bumped into some fool that she wanted to stick up. Starr really didn't feel like doing any robberies tonight. She was really enjoying herself.

"Is everything okay?" Antoine asked in a concerned tone.

Starr slid her phone back into her pocket. "Yes," she answered. "Everything's fine."

Fuck Stevie, Starr thought to herself. She was on one, and Antoine had her undivided attention.

***

"So where are you on your way to now?" Antoine asked after he walked Starr to her car.

Starr unlocked and opened the driver's door. "Home sweet home," she smiled.

Antoine frowned. "I really enjoyed your company today," he said. "I hate to see you go..."

Starr looked down and didn't respond. Actually she didn't know what to say. She enjoyed his company too, but the fact of the matter was she was already taken.

"Antoine...," Starr began.

He slowly tilted her chin upward, and leaned down towards her before planting a soft kiss on Starr's lips.

"I'm...uh...My fault," Antoine quickly apologized. "I know you got someone, it's just...you so cool—but I shouldn't have did that shit. I should've—"

Starr surprised herself when she wrapped her arms around Antoine's neck, and pulled him back down towards her. Her lips crushed against his as she eagerly gave in to her temptation.

Fuck it, she told herself.

Antoine's large hands held her small waist firmly as their tongues danced in unison. Their bodies were pressed so close together that

Starr could feel Antoine's hard dick straining against her through his jeans. Her pussy throbbed in response, and it was obvious that she was turned on.

They finally broke apart only to catch their breaths.

"Do you live close by?" Starr whispered.

"Right around the corner," Antoine answered in a hoarse tone. "You wanna follow me there?"

Starr knew she should have climbed in her car and drove off, but she instead found herself nodding her head.

***

Antoine lived in the Reserve Square Apartments on 12th street. The drive there was less than five minutes, and they were inside his apartment kissing and touching in less than two minutes.

An alcoholic buzz mixed with good conversation had the two of them feeling some type of way as they went at it. Antoine and Starr multi-tasked between making out and undressing as they hastily made their way towards his bedroom.

Clothes were strewn across the floor of the living room, and the moment they reached the bedroom, they both collapsed onto the king size bed.

Starr felt a combination of excitement and anxiety. It had been so long since she had experienced something new and different. The last time she had sex with a guy was in high school which was many years ago. Her heart hammered in her chest.

"Let me get this condom," he said reaching in the drawer of his nightstand.

After rolling the rubber down his dick, he leaned down and kissed Starr once again. "Turn over for me baby," he whispered.

Starr did as she was told, positioning herself on her hands and knees and tooting her ass up seductively.

Antoine took hold of her curvy hips and slid inside her drenched pussy.

"*Oooohhh*, shit," Starr whimpered upon his entrance.

Antoine firmly gripped her waist, pulling her into his strong humps. The sound of skin slapping was the only sound in the room besides Starr's soft moans and Antoine's harsh breathing.

PAP!

The condom suddenly broke!

"Damn," Antoine cursed pulling out. He quickly snatched the punctured rubber off and tossed it to the floor.

Starr's ass was still tooted up as she wondered why he had stopped and pulled out. She didn't hear the condom break.

Antoine hurriedly searched through the nightstand's drawer, but unfortunately that was the last Magnum.

"What are you doing?" Starr whined. "Why did you stop? Put it back in…"

Antoine knew he shouldn't have, but damn if Starr's light skinned ass didn't look good tooted seductively up in the air.

"Fuck it," Antoine told himself as he slid back inside Starr unprotected.

"Damn, Antoine," Star cried. "This feels so good…"

"You feel so nice," Antoine moaned. "I want this to be mine…" His pelvis slammed harshly against Starr's backside. Her breasts bounced and swung back and forth with each powerful stroke that Antoine inflicted.

In a sudden swift movement, Antoine turned Starr over onto her backside. He lifted her left leg over his shoulder and slid deep inside her.

"Oh, shit! Fuck me Antoine!" Starr cried out.

He took hold of one of her breasts and massaged a hardened nipple. His pace sped up once he felt himself approaching a powerful orgasm. He couldn't hold it any longer, Starr was just too damn wet and tight.

"Starr...," Antoine groaned. "I'm about to cum..."

Starr reached down and began massaging her swollen clit. She wanted to cum with him.

Antoine's dick jerked wildly as his thick nut spurted inside Starr. "Mmm...," he groaned. "Damn..."

Starr came shortly after.

Antoine collapsed beside Starr. She couldn't believe what she had just done but it was too late to take it back now.

Antoine wrapped a strong arm around Starr's body and pulled her close. She actually found herself enjoying the warm gesture. Before either of them was able to feel a sense of regret, they suddenly dozed off.

20

"Man, where the fuck is this bitch at?!" Stevie yelled. She kept looking at her phone expecting Starr to call or at least text back, but to Stevie's disappointment she did neither. "Fuck it!" Stevie said. "I'll do this shit myself."

Stevie pulled the black ski mask over her face, and climbed out her car. She stealthily crept across the street, her hand on her piece.

Stevie was hoping she could pull off the stick up with Starr, since Starr was effortlessly able to lead the men right into the unexpected robbery but obviously, Starr was preoccupied. With what exactly Stevie had no idea.

The guy Stevie was planning on robbery was just some young punk from the hood who felt he could floss in the club without anyone noticing. Hell, Stevie did. She kept her eyes on niggas all night waiting for one to slip up so she could pounce on them like a predator to its prey.

The young guy made his way back towards his car which was a black Monte Carlo on twenty-four inch rims. He was on his cell phone texting some chick who had left the club an hour earlier with her girls. He was so pre-occupied with getting some pussy that he didn't even notice Stevie creeping up on him.

Stevie suddenly took off running as she charged at him full speed. She suddenly smacked the butt of her gun against the young guy's head.

He instantly dropped onto the ground. The phone landed several feet away.

"Nigga, you know what time it is! Empty them mufuckin' pockets and hand over the jewelry," she ordered.

"Man, what the fuck?!" the guy cried grabbing the back of his head. A knot was quickly beginning to form. "A nigga can't have shit!"

"Save that bullshit for someone who cares!" Stevie snapped. "Hurry the fuck up!" she yelled. "I ain't got all day."

Not wanting to get murked, the guy quickly did as he was told tossing all the jewelry and money towards Stevie's feet.

"Nigga, don't let me catch yo' ass in the streets," he threatened. "You should take that punk ass mask off yo' face!" He challenged. Stevie may have the gun and power, but that didn't stop the guy from talking shit.

Stevie ignored the guy's threats as she bent down to retrieve the money and jewelry he had just tossed at her feet.

Without warning, the guy suddenly lunged at Stevie tackling her to the ground!

"Ooomph!" The back of Stevie's head collided with the concrete.

The guy quickly climbed on top of Stevie and snatched her ski mask off.

"Get the fuck off me!" Stevie spat.

WHAP!

He suddenly punched the shit out of Stevie. The bridge of her nose instantly dislocated causing her nose to twist at an awkward angle.

"Aaahhh!" Stevie cried out in pain. It was the worst pain she had ever experienced in life!

Blood gushed from her nose like CG effects.

The guy suddenly wrapped his large hands around Stevie's throat and proceeded to viciously choke her. Blood seeped from Stevie's nose into her mouth, and she actually began choking on her own thick dark red blood.

"I cannot believe I almost got robbed by a fuckin' bitch!" he yelled strangling Stevie.

The soles of Stevie's tennis shoes scraped against the pavement as she fought to get him off her, but it was no use. He was far stronger than her.

There she was in the parking lot of a small bar located in the hood getting strangled to death by some nigga she had just attempted to rob. Stevie prayed someone would suddenly come and stop this dude from killing her but unfortunately no one came to her rescue, and she had to deal with the repercussions of what she had done.

This is it. This nigga's about to kill me, she thought to herself.

21

"I bet ya lil' butch ass got some tight pussy," he teased.

Stevie tried to hit him in the face, but he grabbed her arm and roughly pinned it on the side of her head. She was definitely not used to being put in this predicament. Usually she was the one overpowering somebody, but unfortunately the tables were now turned.

"How 'bout I find out?" he asked smiling sadistically. "Huh? Would you like that shit?" He suddenly released her arm, and proceeded to unbutton her jeans.

Fuck no!

Stevie's eyes shot wide open in fear. Gagging noises came from her throat, but she couldn't scream, hell, she barely could breathe. If she was lucky enough, maybe he would kill her before he actually got the chance to fuck her.

I'd rather die before I let a nigga stick his dirty ass dick in me, Stevie thought to herself. Ever since she had been raped by her own father at the tender age of ten she vowed that she would never willingly allow a man penetrate her. She would rather take a bullet to the head any day.

Stevie pushed the guy's head away from her, but he effortlessly shook off her weak attempts to push him away.

His hands suddenly rummaged inside her baggy pants and touched the top of her pussy, caressing the dark mass of curly pubic hair.

Stevie was nearly on the verge of losing consciousness, but he suddenly released her throat only to proceed to unbutton his jeans. Stevie quickly used this to her advantage as she punched and kicked him simultaneously. Her closed fist connected with his temple and he immediately rolled off.

Before he had a moment to recuperate, she quickly retrieved the gun lying beside her, jumped to her feet, and cocked the Glock.

POP!

POP!

POP!

Bullets tore through his body! Three landed in his chest, one piercing his heart, and killing him immediately.

There was no hint of fear or regret as Stevie released the bullets into his body. His lifeless body hit the ground immediately, and Stevie started to continue to shoot at his motionless corpse until suddenly she heard nearby footsteps approaching.

Stevie quickly turned to her right where she noticed two females heading towards their car. They stood frozen in fear as they stared directly at Stevie. They wanted to run, but they were seemingly stuck in place unsure of what they should do. Neither women had ever been placed in such a tense situation.

Stevie suddenly aimed the gun at them and squeezed the trigger!

Both women screamed in fear!

Click!

Click!

The gun chamber was empty. "Fuck," Stevie cursed before running off towards her car. She quickly jumped in and skirted off. Words couldn't describe how pissed she was that the nigga actually had the audacity to touch her.

Stevie couldn't help but feel like all this shit wouldn't have happened if Starr would have been there and doing what the fuck she was supposed.

Stevie floored the gas and got as far away from the scene as she could. "Wait til I get my fuckin' hands on this bitch!" she screamed before punching the center of her steering wheel.

***

The sunlight peeking into Antoine's room shined bright on Starr's face. Her eyelids slowly opened. Antoine lay fast asleep beside her. His arm was still draped over her waist as if they were long time lovers.

Starr slowly lifted his arm, and climbed out of bed. She then checked her cell phone for any missed calls or text messages. Of course, there were several missed calls from Stevie and even a few text messages, one that stood out the most was: *Bitch, where ever you at stay there, cuz if you come home, Ima kill ya ass.*

"I ain't stuttin' this bitch," Starr thought to herself. She then proceeded to dress.

Antoine slowly stirred in bed and sat up as he noticed Starr dressing. "Morning," he greeted in a muffled voice.

"Good morning," Starr said with her back turned to him as she pulled on her leggings. Understandably, she was feeling ashamed of what she had done last night. However, it was far too late to take it back now.

"Are you leaving?" he asked slightly disappointed.

"Yep," Starr answered flatly.

"I don't have classes today," Antoine said. "I was hoping I could take you to breakfast—"

"Antoine, look," Starr turned to face him. "You're a nice guy...," she told him. "You really are but—"

"But you're already with someone," he cut her off. "I can understand and respect that. My bad for even suggesting it."

Starr sighed. She felt bad but it was what it was. She pulled her combat boots on and stood to her feet.

She started to say something to Antoine, but she didn't quite know what to say exactly so she left without uttering another word.

***

"Where the fuck was you last night?" Stevie sat on the sofa with a pissed off look on her face.

She was obviously upset, and couldn't wait for Starr's trifling ass to walk through the front door. As a matter of fact, she didn't a get a lick of sleep last night. Instead she sat on the living room sofa waiting for Starr's sorry as to return home.

Stevie's nose was red and swollen twice its normal size. She had snapped her nose back into place on her own last night since she didn't want to risk going to the hospital. The two chicks that had seen her face had her pretty much shook.

"I—I stayed the night with Diamond in the hospital," Starr lied as she closed the door behind herself. It was funny how easily Starr could lie to niggas but every time she tried to with Stevie, she failed miserably.

"Bitch, you lyin' and I know it," Stevie said. "I see right through ya ass. Now I'ma ask you again," she began. "Where the fuck was you at last night?"

"I told you I was—"

Stevie suddenly leapt off the couch and ran full speed towards Starr slamming her against the front door! Starr's purse immediately dropped onto the hardwood floors.

"Hoe, you think I'm fuckin' stupid?!" Stevie screamed. She quickly snatched down Starr's leggings and shoved her lace panties to the side.

Without warning, Stevie jammed two fingers inside Starr's sore, dry pussy.

"Stevie, what that the fuck are you doing?!" Starr cried. "That shit hurts! *Stop*!"

Stevie ignored Starr's cries as she continued to assault Starr's pussy with her fingers. Starr finally managed to shove Stevie off her after several attempts.

Stevie lifted her fingers towards her nostrils and sniffed them. "Bitch, you been fuckin!" she screamed.

"You're fucking crazy!" Starr argued. "I don't know what the hell you talkin' about!" She tried to walk around Stevie, but Stevie suddenly shoved Starr back against the door.

"Bitch, smell this shit!" Stevie yelled jamming her fingers in Starr's face. "Smell it!"

"Get the fuck away from me, Stevie!" Starr yelled.

"Hoe, I can smell that nigga's dick!" Stevie screamed.

Starr pushed Stevie off of her and ran into the bathroom locking the door behind herself.

"I can't fuckin' believe you!" Stevie yelled out. "I was getting my ass kicked last night! *I needed you!* And what were you doing?!" Stevie asked. "You were getting fucked by some nigga in the streets."

Starr plopped down onto the toilet seat and began crying hysterically.

Stevie slowly made her way towards the bathroom door. There was no way in hell she was going to let up about the shocking revelation she had just discovered. "You ain't shit Starr Renee!" she yelled. "You say you love me! You say you'll never put a nigga over me! But you a fuckin' lie! I hope it was worth it, bitch!" she screamed. Stevie was obviously hurt by Starr's actions. She couldn't believe her beloved girlfriend would betray her.

"Just leave me alone, Stevie!" Starr yelled.

"Leave you alone?!" Stevie repeated in disbelief. "Oh, you want me to leave you alone now, huh?" she asked. "Kinda like how you left me alone last night to get some dick?!" Stevie laughed sadistically. "But you know what?" she said. "It's all good bitch...cuz guess what? I been fuckin' with ya girl, Diamond. How you like that shit, bitch?"

Starr immediately ceased her crying. It felt as if her breath had just caught in her chest as she listened to Stevie's shocking news. She had to be hearing shit! She just had to be!

"I see ya mufuckin' ass quiet now!" Stevie chuckled. "Yeah, you heard right. I been fucking with Diamond for quite some now."

"You fuckin' lyin', Stevie!" Starr screamed. "Just shut that shit up!" Starr didn't believe for one second that Diamond would betray her like that. Nah...not Diamond. Not her best friend

Diamond. Stevie was only trying to get back at her by using her friend against her.

"Oh, you think I'm lying?!" Starr yelled through the closed bathroom door. "Well how would I know that Diamond's clit is pierced?!"

Starr's heart felt like it had sank to the pit of her stomach. Diamond and Starr had gone to get piercings together. Starr had gotten her tongue done while Diamond had gotten her clit pierced.

"And how would I know that when I'm sucking on her pussy, it gets way wetter than yours—"

Starr jumped off the toilet seat and swung the bathroom door open. Stevie quickly backed out of the way since she expected Starr to start swinging. However, Starr surprised her when she walked right past Stevie and headed towards the front door.

"Yo, where the fuck you going?!" Stevie yelled out after Starr.

Starr ignored Stevie's question as she reached down, grabbed her purse and walked out the front door slamming it behind herself.

22

Starr burst inside Diamond's hospital room. Her friend was watching Judge Joe Brown and eating lunch which consisted of a pepperoni pizza, mixed fruit, and a stale oatmeal cookie.

"Please tell me Stevie's lying!" Starr blurted out.

Diamond looked at Starr like she was crazy. "Bitch, what the fuck are you talking about?" she asked in a calm tone. "And what the hell got your panties in a bunch?"

"You and Stevie?" Starr asked. "Is it true? Ya'll been fucking each other behind my back?!"

Diamond's mouth fell open. So the cat was finally out of the bag. She never thought that dirt would be revealed.

"Don't just sit there looking stupid, hoe!" Starr yelled. "Answer me!"

Diamond was at a loss for words for a moment. She didn't know what exactly to say. Hell, she never thought this moment would come. After all her and Stevie had made it perfectly clear that Starr was to never find out about the shit they were doing together on the side.

"Shit, Starr! You act like you don't know the type of bitch Stevie is!" Diamond yelled. It was a half assed way for her to defend herself.

"Bitch, this ain't about Stevie! This about you!" Starr screamed. "So it's true then?! You and Stevie were really fucking around?!"

"Yes! Okay? Yes!" Diamond finally admitted.

Starr already figured the shit was probably true, but she needed confirmation from Diamond. She basically needed to hear the shit from the horse's mouth.

"You were supposed to be like my fuckin' sister!" Starr screamed before viciously kicking Diamond's broken leg.

"Aaaaahhh! Fuck!" Diamond yelled in pain.

"Bitch, we done! You ain't shit in my eyes! Don't ever hit me up, hoe! Don't even think about me! Our friendship is over!" With that said Starr left the room.

Diamond's leg throbbed in pain. "Shit," she cursed. "The fuck just happened?" she asked herself.

It seemed like everything in her life was just falling apart slowly but surely.

***

Rich came to visit Diamond that afternoon. She barely even looked up and acknowledged his presence or the bundle of roses and the teddy bear he was holding as he entered her hospital room.

"How you feelin' lady?" he asked.

"Like shit," Diamond answered in a flat tone. She was obviously still pissed about the shit that had happened earlier.

Rich placed the teddy bear and roses on the table beside the hospital bed and kissed Diamond on the forehead.

"Doctor's ain't come and give you no pain medication?" he asked.

There was no pain medication that could heal the hurt Diamond felt in her heart. Starr and Diamond had never ever even had a verbal argument before so the fact that Starr had just flipped on her really hurt. Who could blame Starr though? They were supposed to be friends and Diamond had done Starr worse than an enemy in the streets.

"It's not that," Diamond muttered. "My girl Starr, she just...she came here...we ended up falling out," she admitted. She barely even wanted to talk about the shit.

Rich took a seat in the chair next to Diamond's hospital bed. He knew that Diamond was expecting to hear some words of comfort from him to lighten the situation about her best friend, but Rich really could give two shits about Starr's ass. "Real shit, you don't need a nigga or a bitch with me in ya life."

***

Starr had left so suddenly that she didn't even realize she had left her cell phone behind. Stevie was in Starr's shit before Starr even exited the apartment building.

As soon as the phone was in Stevie's hands she instantly began snooping through it. The text messages were the first thing she checked since she saw Starr had received a text message not too long ago.

"Who the hell is Ashley?" Stevie asked herself. She didn't recall Starr having a friend by that name.

Stevie anxiously read the text message: *I really enjoyed your company yesterday, but I can also respect that you're in a relationship. The last thing I ever wanna do is disrespect u. Real talk, I would love to see you again but only under your terms...*

Stevie snorted in jealousy. "Ashley my ass," she said to herself. She didn't live as long as she did being a fool. A smile tugged at the corners of Stevie's lips as she texted: *I would love to see you today. Where can I meet you?*

***

Starr brought her car to a slow stop underneath the red light at the intersection. Suddenly, she burst into a fit of hysterical cries unable to hold her emotions in any longer.

"How could this bitch do this shit to me?!" Starr yelled.

Stevie's actions didn't surprise Starr so much as Diamond's. Diamond was supposed to be her girl, her BFF for life.

Starr was finally fed up with Stevie's betrayal. "I'ma show this bitch!" she said wiping her tears away.

23

Where u at, Antoine texted Starr's phone.

He was supposed to be in his African Studies class, but he was playing hookie just to see and talk to Starr. He was really digging her, but he also didn't want to run her away due to the unfortunate circumstances of her having someone.

Antoine stood underneath the bridge on 93rd street. It was such an atypical place to meet someone, but he figured maybe Starr just didn't want anyone around when they spoke.

He decided to call Starr to see where she was. Surprisingly, she didn't answer. Antoine was just about to throw the towel in and leave until he suddenly saw a red 2008 Dodge Charger pull into the broken-up driveway that led under the abandoned bridge.

"That ain't Starr's car," Antoine said to himself.

He tried to peer into the car through the dark tinted windshield but was only able to see a silhouette. Antoine became irritated and uncomfortable all at the same time.

The Charger came to a slow stop, but the engine remained running as the driver gradually stepped out the car.

Antoine stood outside directly in front of his car as he waited for Starr to get out.

Stevie suddenly emerged from the car and pointed her gun towards Antoine. Before he was able to recognize what the hell was going on, Stevie quickly pulled the trigger.

POP!

A single bullet instantly tore through Antoine's chest directly beneath his right collar bone. He stumbled backwards upon the impact of the gunshot and fell against the hood of his car. His eyes widened in disbelief as he looked from Stevie down to the hole in his chest oozing blood.

Stevie quickly made her way over towards Antoine. Gravel crunched beneath the soles of her sneakers. "Nigga, I hope the pussy was worth it," she sneered.

Antoine's breathing became harsh as he slowly felt his life slipping away from his body. What a fucked up way to go out. He had simply run into the wrong woman and fell prey to her unexpected drama.

Antoine coughed up a mouthful of thick dark red blood as he slid down onto the ground.

Stevie raised the barrel of the gun to Antoine's head. "You fucked the wrong bitch, bruh..."

***

Starr hurriedly handed over her documentation to the banker in US Bank. She was withdrawing all of the money from her and Stevie's joint account, and then she was getting far away from Cleveland, Diamond, and Stevie's treacherous ass. Her plan was to run away and never come back. Starr felt like if she didn't do it now then she would never get another opportunity.

Antoine's words kept replaying over and over in her head. *You will never know what you're capable of until you try it.* Starr was finally taking a chance and she prayed it would be well worth it.

24

A Month Later

"I'm not even going to be able to wear half the shit you just brought," Diamond laughed as she and Rich walked through Kenwood Mall in Cincinnati, Ohio.

Diamond had been recently released from the hospital, and Rich was eager to show her just the type of nigga he was.

"Well when you're back on your feet ya ass won't have to worry about shopping for a minute."

Diamond headed towards an empty nearby bench. "Hold up, let's stop right here. I need a quick break," she said in an exasperated tone. She was still getting used to using the crutches.

Rich followed Diamond over towards the bench. He needed an extra arm to carry all the shopping bags Diamond had. The moment they walked through the doors of the upscale mall, and he told her to get whatever, she just didn't know how to act.

Aldo's, Michael Kors, Coach, Bebe, BCBG, Nordstrom's, Express, Dillards, Nine West, Macy's. Rich was on the verge of paying a random motherfucker in the mall just to carry Diamond's many shopping bags.

"You good?" he asked her in that nonchalant tone of his.

Diamond was used to it by now. "Just gotta catch my breath," she told him. "I'll be so happy when I don't gotta use these shits anymore."

Rich joined Diamond on the bench. "A nigga wanna take care of you just like this," he told her. "Shoppin' sprees, expensive vacations, cars...whatever you want. I could make it happen."

Diamond was caught off guard by his proposal. She turned to face him and gave him the side eye. She wanted to see if he was serious but she could tell by his expression that he was.

"Diamond you the type of chick that needs a nigga to take care of her for the rest of her life," Rich said. "I ain't no slow nigga," he explained. "I could look at ya ass and tell that shit. You used to a nigga payin' yo' way through life. Now the thing about me is...I don't mind doin' that shit. But I ain't no fuckin' trick...and you gon' have to play ball..."

"Play ball?" Diamond asked curiously. "What do you mean by that?"

"You my number one draft pick. You gon' always have all you want and need, but you gotta play yo' position. As long as I ain't worried about whose team you on you ain't gotta worry about a thing. Simple as that."

***

"Be careful," Diamond whispered in a nervous tone.

Rich kissed her passionately as he positioned himself between her thighs. "I told you I promise I'ma be careful with you, ma. I would never wanna hurt you."

Diamond whimpered as Rich slid inside her awaiting pussy. Her legs were spread far apart and her left leg sat elevated on a plush pillow.

Rich wished he could have been patient enough to wait until Diamond was fully healed, but a nigga had needs and he had waited long enough to slide up in her shit. He was going hard for her and he didn't even know if the pussy was good or not.

Diamond's fingernails dug into Rich's back as he filled her with slow and steady strokes. Fortunately, he now knew.

"Remember what I told ya ass," he said. "This my pussy...you understand me?"

"Yes," Diamond moaned.

Rich went a little deeper. "Yes what?" he asked.

"God!" Diamond bellowed. "Yes Rich! Yes, daddy! *Fuck me!*"

"You mine," Rich said. "You hear me? You're mine..."

***

Rich had continued to hold Diamond down much like he had promised. The side chicks were now strictly forbidden to come to Rich's home now that Diamond had a permanent spot there. Rich caked her better than any trick she had ever messed with, and Diamond still couldn't figure out what Rich's aim was. Sure, she knew he considered her his ole lady, but she still didn't know why he had chosen her when he had could have chosen any chick he wanted to.

Aside from paying her medical bills, Rich also paid for the repairs of her BMW, the city damages, and even paid the past due rent on her apartment since her licks didn't fall through due to her hospital stay.

Rich Keys was the perfect 'cuffing material', but getting serious with him was actually the last thing on Diamond's mind regardless of the shit she had agreed to. Instead she was trying to figure out what all she could get out of his ass and then leave him high and dry.

One thing about Diamond that Rich failed to realize was that she was a hoe, plain and simple. Once a hoe always a hoe, and if he thought he could impress her enough to be wifey then he had a whole other thing coming. The saying was as goes: You cannot turn a hoe into a housewife and the case was evident with Diamond.

One evening while Rich was at Fantasy's Gentlemen's Club, Diamond had decided to do some much-needed snooping around. Her leg was still in its healing process, but she now wore a knee brace around her knee instead of a cast.

Limping around his huge home, she began looking around and trying to find a safe if he had one. Yeah, it was 2013 and most people kept their money in a bank, but true hustlers never kept all their eggs in one basket.

Diamond searched Rich's home high low, looking in every nook and cranny for a safe. Her hope slowly dissipated when she unfortunately didn't come across it as fast as she thought she would.

Diamond was on the verge of tossing the towel in until she finally noticed a slightly crooked picture frame on the dining room wall. Feeling her hope quickly return, Diamond hurriedly snatched the frame off the wall and carefully placed it on the hardwood floors. As expected there was a small space in the wall and nestled in the center was a compact safe. Diamond anxiously snatched it out, walked over towards the dining room table and placed the safe down.

It was a digital safe, and Diamond pretty much knew how to crack those flimsy things open. She didn't get too excited about the amount of money inside because for the one the safe was very small, and the quality of the safe was pretty cheap.

Without further ado, she hit the top of the safe and turned the dial simultaneously. At the first attempt, the safe didn't budge but the second time she executed the two step move the door popped right open for her.

Inside the safe had to be no more than thirty thousand dollars, but Diamond quickly snatched that up, placed the safe back inside its designated hiding place and proceeded to gather her belongings.

She had played the "wifey" role for far long enough already, but now it was time to get back to her world. There was too much money to be made, and she was missing out on it playing wifey to Rich's ass.

Diamond was a money hungry bitch and she was damn proud of it. Her love of cash was what fueled her greed.

After gathering up her belongings, and quickly dressing, Diamond decided to call a cab to pick her up. Her car was still in the repair shop—and would remain there until her frame was fully repaired—and even when it was fixed, she wasn't quite sure if she was ready to hop back behind the wheel of a car so soon. Hell, she still had nightmares about the accident.

Diamond anxiously limped towards the front door determined to get ghost before Rich finally returned and discovered his precious money was gone.

Diamond pulled her purse over her shoulder and reached for the handle of the front door—suddenly, it swung open before she even had a chance to turn the knob.

Diamond's breathing felt like it had suddenly caught in her chest as her heart dropped to the pit of her stomach. Standing less than a foot from her was Rich who wore a smug expression on his chocolate face.

"Where you going Diamond?" he asked with a confused look on his face.

Diamond may have been tripping, but the question seemed more like a statement almost as if he was shocked she was actually leaving his home to begin with.

"I was...um...I—uh," Diamond stuttered.

"You don't look so good bay," Rich noted, eyeing the tiny specks of sweat on Diamond's forehead.

"No...I...um...I feel...um..."

Rich reached out to touch Diamond's wet forehead, and she instantly flinched at his raised hand.

"Relax, bay," Rich chuckled. He then stepped inside the home and Diamond backed up. After closing the door, he stared suspiciously at Diamond. "What the hell is up with you?" he asked.

"I—nothing—I'm cool. Why do you ask?"

"Come on now," Rich said matter-of-factly. "A nigga ain't live this long being no fool," he told her. "What's up with you?"

"I swear, nothing! Everything is fine," Diamond even forced a phony smile to further convince him.

"Diamond, what did I tell you when I first started fuckin' heavy with you?" he asked. "I told you you can get whatever you want from me, but to just keep it real..."

"I...I...uh...."

Rich shook his head. He figured that he would just find out for himself. Suddenly, his tuition le him towards his safe.

Diamond watched in horror as he headed towards the dining room. *Run bitch*, she told herself. *Move your ass and run.*

Who was she kidding, her leg was fucked up. How in the hell was she going to run anywhere?

Rich made his way inside the dining room and quickly noticed something was out of the ordinary. Diamond's dumb ass didn't even bother replacing the picture frame on the wall.

Diamond's feet were seemingly glued to the floor. Her brain was telling her to flee, but her body wouldn't cooperate.

Rich's mouth fell open. "*Bitch, what the fuck*?!" he yelled.

Diamond finally gathered up enough courage to try to run out the front door, but Rich suddenly rushed her and snatched her up by her Peruvian weave before she was able to even touch the doorknob.

"Bitch, I oughta beat yo' mothafuckin' ass! Stealing from me after all the shit I done for yo' ungrateful ass!" He brutally dragged her towards the bathroom. "Don't worry, I got somethin' worse in store for your ass!"

"Rich, I'm sorry!" Diamond cried. Her purse and belongings dropped out of her hands as she reached for her hair.

"Yeah, you're right!" Rich agreed. "You are a sorry ass bitch!"

Once inside the main level's bathroom, Rich shoved Diamond against the sink, roughly turned her around so that her back faced him, and snatched her jeans down her legs.

"Rich, please, I'm sorry!" Diamond cried. Tears streamed down her cheeks.

"Shut that shit up! I don't wanna hear that bullshit now!" Rich cursed. He roughly bent Diamond over the sink, spit into the palm of his hand and rubbed the saliva between her ass cheeks.

He then unbuttoned his jeans and snatched them below his waist before pulling his dick out. Without warning, he jammed his dick inside Diamond's tight asshole.

"*Aaaahhh!*" she screamed out in excruciating pain. The agony was almost unbearable. She could feel the skin around her rectum tearing upon his painful entrance and the fact that it was barely lubricated didn't help matters in the least.

Rich forced Diamond upward and made her look at herself in the mirror as he brutally fucked her in the ass.

"This is what I do to sneaky hoes I can't trust!" he spat.

"I'm sorry...," Diamond squeaked out. Saliva dripped from her mouth as she cried and thick mucus oozed from both her nostrils.

She tried to put her head down because she didn't want to look at her own reflection, but Rich yanked her head back by her hair forcing her to look at what he was doing to her.

"I tried to do the right thing with ya ass, but now this is all you mean to me now bitch! You hear me?" His strokes got harder and more aggressive as he pounded into her asshole.

It felt as if someone had lit a flame and held it near her anus. The pain was just too much.

"You lil' trifling ass bitch!" he cursed. "Look at you! Look at yourself, hoe. Look at what you are you lil' fuckin' bitch!"

Diamond's bloodcurdling screams reverberated off the walls of the bathroom.

25

Diamond's finger's twitched and her entire body seemed to be trembling as she sat on the edge of Rich's bed. Her ass was on fire, her mind was in shambles and she felt like nothing.

Suddenly, Rich emerged from the steamy master bathroom with a terry cloth towel wrapped around his waist. He had to wash the shit and blood off his dick, but he knew without a doubt that his point had been proven.

Diamond's dry lips trembled as she continued to stare at the carpet. She was totally out of it.

Rich didn't even look in Diamond's direction as he walked over towards his dresser and pulled out a pair of Hanes Boxer.

"What are you gonna do to me now?" Diamond whispered, barely audible. Her eyes were still glued to the carpet as she spoke. She was scared shitless.

Rich turned and faced Diamond after he pulled his boxers up. "What?" he asked in a nasty tone. "Come again?"

Diamond slowly looked up at Rich. Her eyes were watery and there was an awkward look about her. She definitely didn't look like herself. "I said," she began in a slightly louder tone. "What are you gonna do to me now?"

Rich proceeded to pull on a pair of True Religions. "I don't know what the fuck I'ma do with ya ass," he said in a nonchalant tone, not even looking at her. "I'm still thinkin' about it. Maybe I'll go for a round two tonight..."

Just the thought of Rich penetrating her swollen ass again had her feeling squeamish. She couldn't take any more punishment.

"Please, no...," Diamond quickly said.

"Please, no what Diamond?" Rich asked. "Please, no what?" He turned to face her. "I kill mufuckas for the shit you did to me earlier—"

"What if," Diamond paused and looked at the ground.

"What if what?!" Rich barked.

Diamond's eyes slowly lifted as she met Rich's intense gaze. "What if I told you I know who killed your brother...?"

PRETTY YOUNG THINGS 2 IS NOW AVAILABLE!

EXCERPT FROM "*I FELL IN LOVE WITH A REAL STREET THUG*"

1

KHARI

PRESENT DAY

With my 7-year old son Ali in tow, I carefully made my way to the visits hall where my fiancé awaited our arrival. This was only Ali's third time visiting his father in prison, because I hated him having to see his dad locked up. Normally, I didn't bring him with me to visitation but Aubrey insisted. He claimed his family was the only thing keeping him sane behind prison walls, so I refused to rob him of the privilege of being a father to his only child.

When me and Ali entered the somewhat noisy hall, we found Aubrey sitting alone at an empty stainless steel table, surrounded by fellow inmates and their chatty relatives. My smile widened as I approached him and he graciously returned it. He had a fresh cut and his face was groomed. It was nice to see that he was taking care of himself. I couldn't front. Even for a convicted felon, Aubrey looked good.

At 35, he was ten years older than me,

dark chocolate, and somewhat rough around the edges. He had big, brown eyes, long lashes, and thick, juicy lips. There was a small scar along his jaw and one that ran through his left eyebrow that he told me was from a bar fight years ago.

Flaws aside, Aubrey was devilishly handsome. Slim, tall, and toned in build, he reminded me of an NBA player in his prime. Aubrey had always been a gym rat and he made sure it showed in his physique.

Covering over 60% of his body was a collage of decorative tattoos. The only areas that weren't tatted was his face and neck. His favorite one of all was the portrait of Ali on his upper arm. Our son was his proudest accomplishment.

Aubrey quickly stood to his feet to greet us. "*Waa gwaan, empress*," he said in a thick Caribbean accent. He was born and raised in St. Thomas and relocated to the U.S. ten years ago. "It's been a minute since I seen ya'll." Pulling me and Ali towards him, Aubrey hugged us tightly. It'd been almost four months to be exact, and although I wanted to see him more, work and school simply wouldn't permit it. Taking time off for the 3 ½ hour drive from Atlanta to Savannah was easier said than done.

"I tried to get out here last week but my schedule was hectic—"

"Guess what? You here though. That's all

that matters. Not to mention, I had to prepare myself mentally before we linked up."

I could respect that he wanted to have his mind right before he dealt with me. We all took our respectful seats, with Ali sitting closest to Aubrey. He was unashamedly a daddy's boy since Aubrey spoiled him. Ali gave a snaggle-tooth grin after his father playfully ruffled his short, curly hair. He had my hazel eyes, coffee complexion, and dimpled chin. Everyone said that he was a spitting image of me.

"So...how are you holding up?" I asked. It was nearly two years since Aubrey was arrested on drug and weapon charges. This was his third strike, so the judge and jury didn't cut him any slack at trial. I almost fainted in court when they read his sentencing. Ever since he'd left, my life just hadn't been the same.

"Same shit, different day."

Ali excitedly communicated through hand gestures. He was born with congenital hearing loss due to pregnancy complications. Aubrey never wanted Ali to feel different from other children so he overindulged when it came to spoiling him. Our son had all of the latest high tech gadgets, game consoles, and every special edition shoe known to man. Aubrey cherished his son and spared no expense when it came to him. He was a damn good father, which was why I'd stayed with him for as long as I did, in spite of his constant infidelities.

Prior to his imprisonment, Aubrey had a real problem with keeping his dick in his pants. As a well-known music producer and party host, he was always surrounded by aspiring models, artists, and thirsty hoes looking for a quick come up. There were some side chicks out there willing to do anything for the limelight. It wasn't until I threatened to leave him for good that Aubrey finally straightened up his act and proposed to me.

"Ali just said he misses you a lot." Since Aubrey was always in the streets or at the studio, he never bothered to learn sign language. Luckily for him, Ali was an expert when it came to reading lips. "Sometimes he wakes up thinking that you're still there," I told him. "Sometimes I do too..."

"You know you gotta nigga deep in his feelings about ya'll," Aubrey said. Pulling his son close, he kissed the top of his head.

It was a few weeks until Christmas and I hated that he wouldn't be home for the holidays. I could tell he was saddened that he couldn't physically be there for us.

"Have you heard anything from the lawyer?" I asked, changing the subject. We'd been working on an appeal ever since his conviction.

Aubrey scoffed and rolled his eyes. He hated whenever I brought up legal matters during visitation. "Nah...but don't trouble yaself about it, y' hear? A real nigga gon' stand where a real nigga land. As long as my family's good I ain't gon' ever lose sleep."

"Aubrey, by the time you get out your son will practically be an adult," I reminded him. "How could you sleep peacefully knowing that you'll miss out on him growing up?"

"You said the key thing...when I get out. You know they can't keep a real nigga down for long. I'mma still be there for him no matter what."

"How can you be there for him when you're in here?!" I yelled.

With a concerned expression, Ali asked if I were okay. He wasn't accustomed to seeing me lose my cool, and I prided myself on my patience. Simmering down a bit before I caused a scene, I raked a hand through my naturally curly hair and sighed. I hated for my son to see me worked up but our current state of affairs was ultimately taking its toll on me. Aubrey had been gone for over a year and I still wasn't used to his absence. Forcing a smile, I told Ali that I was fine in sign language.

He had no idea that it was a lie.

In fact, I was gradually falling apart. I

never anticipated on raising our child alone. Because I had grown up in a two parent household, I wanted the same for our son. And as thankful as I was for the lifestyle Aubrey gave us, I would've chosen him over it any day.

Sensing my frustrations, he reached over and placed his hand over mine. The simple gesture alone made me relax a little. Aubrey had a knack for making me feel secure.

I met Aubrey while waitressing part-time at a family owned diner. I'd just started my freshman year in college and needed the extra money for books. He and his brother visited one day during lunch hours. They'd only been living in the states for three months at the time of our introduction.

Truthfully, I didn't immediately find Aubrey attractive. He was scruffy looking, overly confident, and a tad bit aggressive. But over time, I grew to love everything about him. He helped mold me into the woman I was today. He taught me a lot, and he was the first and only man I'd ever truly loved. With that being said, I eventually got over the crush I had on Cue. He moved to New York just before I went off to school and I never saw him again.

"I'm locked up, but my money ain't. You think these bars gon' stop a nigga from getting money? These bars ain't stopping shit. If anything, these bars taught me how to network better," he explained. "Can't shit stop me from taking care of my family."

There was a long period of silence between us before he spoke again.

"You still be in the church every Sunday?" Aubrey asked.

I'd been attending the Sunday services at our local church devotedly. I even helped organize some of the special events. "Yes," I answered. "Every week."

"Aight, then have faith that shit's gon' get greater later."

Something about his words gave me hope. And he was right. He really did do everything he could to take care of his family. He may've been imprisoned, but his revenue consistently poured in like he was still in the streets.

Aubrey ran a lucrative drug business outside of his music career. He even he had a few loyal customers that were in the industry. Every month, he received packages that were shipped to different people's houses, and the niggas on his payroll sold the work on the streets.

Aubrey never had that shit around us; he never even had a shipment delivered to our house. He didn't want us exposed to his lifestyle, and I was fine with that because I'd never condoned him selling drugs in the first place.

Since it was our main source of income I couldn't quite complain either. After all, it was the same money that funded my education.

Mama would've been so disappointed if she ever found out the truth about Aubrey. I had told her that he was arrested for failing to pay taxes. She didn't know about his life as a dealer. For years she'd been under the impression that he was nothing more than a music producer. Mama would've shunned me if she knew I'd fallen in love with a criminal.

As much as I wanted to confide in her, I knew that I couldn't. Mama already wasn't too fond Aubrey because of the issues I'd spoken to her about in the past. I mean, how could she respect a man who constantly lied, cheated, and abused her daughter?

Mama told me time and time again to leave him alone but I just couldn't. Honestly, this street shit and Aubrey's thugged out mentality turned me on. He made me feel important, like I was that bitch. Not to mention, he laid it down like a beast in the bedroom. He had me so gone that I didn't want to return. He had me sprung like a box mattress. Everything about him captivated me.

Aubrey was street, but he was also wise, patient, and clever. Being with him was like a breath of fresh air. Because he was older, he was a lot more mature than the young fuck boys I used to entertain. He'd gotten me at a young age and groomed me into the woman and mother I was today.

Shaking off those worrisome feelings, I caressed his hand and smiled. "I'll try to have faith..." It was the best I could come up with.

Aubrey sensed my uncertainty. "You can't try to have faith. You gotta *believe*," he stressed.

After several minutes of small talk and reminiscing, a C.O. finally notified everyone that visiting hours were over. Ali sulked and pouted since we had to leave, but I reminded him that we'd be back next month.

When Aubrey pulled me in for a firm, farewell hug, he whispered in my ear, "Make sure you keep things in line. We don't need you falling off track."

I knew exactly what he meant by that. "Aubrey, I'm too busy working and raising your son to be out here entertaining other men."

"That's real, stay focused," he said. "Do you think you can do me a favor though? You think you can cover my shit up next time you come here...'fore I have to *kill* one of these niggas." Out of nowhere, Aubrey snapped on one of his fellow inmates. "*Wah di bumboclaat wrang wid yu!?*" I assumed the man was from the islands as well since he'd started speaking broken English. The older man had been checking me out ever since I walked in.

"How 'bout I just wear a black trash bag instead," I said sarcastically.

Aubrey squeezed my ass and pulled me towards him. "Alright now," he said as if he were warning me. "*Mmm.*" He gave my butt another firm squeeze and Ali quickly covered his eyes. He never cared to see our affection. "Dat mufucka back there gettin' fat," he teased. "I'mma have to make a way to get up in that. So the next time you come make sure you don't have no panties on."

With a flirtatious grin, I told him, "How about we just focus on one thing at a time."

Thankfully, my chubbiness transitioned into a curvy and voluptuous shape. I rocked a size sixteen with pride, but the extra weight was in all the right places. Everyone said that I had Ali to thank for that.

"Alright, queen." Aubrey kissed my forehead. Tilting my chin up to meet his gaze, he stared lovingly into my eyes. "I don't wanna have to wait long to see that pretty smile again."

"I promise you won't."

Aubrey ruffled his son's hair again before giving him a final hug. After saying our goodbyes, we parted ways.

"Bless up yaself," Aubrey called after me.

Right about now, I needed all of the blessings I could get if I planned on holding him down for this ten-year stretch. Looking down at my son, I suddenly had doubts about marrying a man in prison.

Would things get better? Would things get worse?

I had no idea how to cope with this shit and I wasn't sure where my life was going. Not to mention, I had a child to think about. It wasn't fair for me to drag him through this shit. Men could make things sound really good at rehearsal, but the outcome could be entirely different.

All of a sudden, I began to have doubts about everything in general. It was the first time since Aubrey's conviction that I actually questioned myself as well as my moralities.

2

KYLIE

I got broads in Atlanta...

Twisting dope, lean, and the Fanta...

Credit cards and scammers...

Hitting off licks in the bando...

Black X6, Phantom...

White X6 looks like a panda...

Going out like I'm Montana...

Hundred killers, hundred hammers...

My best friend Paige multi-tasked between twerking and smoking a blunt to Desiigner's *Panda*. She was a cute, slender Puerto-Rican girl, originally from the Flatbush area of Brooklyn, New York.

Paige was my partner in crime. We'd met in jail a couple years back and were both there for petty theft. Everyone—including my sister—thought she was a bad influence but I didn't give a fuck. I was a grown ass woman, free to make my own choice in friends.

Just then, Paige took off her leggings to watch her booty jiggle and shake in the full length mirror. Her pink Hello Kitty draws were riding insanely high up her ass while she danced but she obviously thought that shit was cute. Paige was a ho, who'd seen more cocks than the walls of a sperm bank.

Thankfully, my bedroom door was closed. I knew how much the trap music and smell of weed bothered mama. Also, she wasn't particularly fond of Paige. She and Khari loved pretending they were holier than thou. They never liked my men, friends, or lifestyle. Oh well, fuck 'em.

At 25, I was still living at home. After losing the baby at 7 months, I just gave up on most shit in life, including independence. Khari went on to get a degree and have a kid while I pretty much stayed stagnant. The miscarriage had fucked me all the way up. I'd even started popping Percocet and stealing again just to fill the void inside of me. No one was happier than me about the pregnancy...and when my son died, I just lost it. I lost myself.

"What do you think about me getting ass shots?" Paige asked, interrupting my thoughts.

"Hoe, I'm thinking about that yeast infection you finna be stuck with. Anyway, we need to be focused on *making* money instead of spending it," I reminded her. "Speaking of which, how much you think we can get for all this shit?"

Laid across my mattress was all of the designer purses, expensive perfumes, and clothes we'd stolen from Nordstrom's a few hours earlier. Boosting had become my way of life.

Paige took a final puff on the blunt before passing it to me. "Hmm..." She looked over every item carefully while doing the math in her head. "Roughly, I'd say...close to a grand."

I sighed exasperatedly. "*Ugh*! That's it?! Bitch, I need a lick! Not this chump change we been making. I'm tired of Uber and riding the fucking bus. I need a car, bitch." The days of borrowing money from mama were over since I'd burned my bridges there. I had to make sure I was able to support me by any means necessary.

Paige placed a finger on her chin like she was thinking. "If we try to upsell—"

"*Upsell*?! Bitch, ain't nobody 'bout to spend big money on some yoga pants and Michael Kors bags. See, I told ya ass we should've hit one of them luxury stores like Gucci or Celine. But noooo, you ain't want to—"

"Dummy, that shit be secured as fuck. Plus, they got cameras like a mothafucka—"

"Lock-picking is my forte...and fuck a camera. I'll wear a hoodie or something," I argued. "Them bitches be running a couple grand easy. We could rack up a few thousands apiece with no sweat if we snagged a few."

"I don't know," Paige said, doubtfully. "Shit, I'm all for making a come up, but ain't nobody trying to go to jail. Hell, I just *got off* probation."

"Hoe, ain't *nobody* going to jail."

"Well, I say you go for it and let me know how that works out."

I rolled my eyes at Paige and shook my head. Sometimes she could be such a pussy. "You real crusty for that shit."

She opened her mouth to say something but was interrupted by the doorbell ringing. I almost expected mama to answer until I remembered that she and her boyfriend, Lenny were on a three-day cruise in the Bahamas. "All I'm asking is for you to think about it. Okay?" I said on my way out the room.

Padding barefoot to the front door, I stood on my tiptoes and looked through the peephole. Much to my surprise, there was no one standing on the other end. "What the hell?"

Chalking it up to some bad ass kids in the 'hood, I turned and walked away—

Ding dong.

Growling in frustration, I stomped back to

the front of the house. When I looked through the peephole again there was still no one there. Fed up with the bullshit, I swung the door open in anger. "Look, whoever the fuck is playing on my gotdamn—"

All of a sudden, someone reached out and grabbed me.

3

KYLIE

A calloused hand clamped tightly over my mouth before I could scream for help. As I struggled in my captor's embrace, I felt his erection pressing into the small of my back. *Oh my God, this nigga about to rape me*! My throat stung as I desperately tried to call Paige's name. It was useless since my mouth was covered.

When I recognized who was holding me I finally calmed down. "Jamaal! You fucking asshole!" Never in a million years did I expect to see my ex. Then again, he had a habit of coming out the cut like Cosby victims.

Whap!

I hit him as hard as I could in the chest as he laughed hysterically like seeing me scared was the funniest shit on earth.

"It's not funny, Jamaal! You childish as fuck!"

Whap!

I hit him again, this time across his face. In one fluid motion, he grabbed my wrist and snatched me so close to him that our bodies were pressed together.

"That rough shit only makes my dick hard."

Disgusted by his words and mere presence, I pushed him away. "Boy, I wouldn't fuck you or any nigga that resembles you. And why the hell do you play so much? You almost gave me a damn heart attack! What is wrong with you? I seriously could've hurt you—"

"Man, hold that noise and gimme that tongue to suck on."

Jamaal leaned in to kiss me but I quickly moved away. *"Hell naw!* I don't know where the fuck your tongue been. Besides, it ain't even that type of party no more, Mall. It's been years since I last saw you. You always in and out. You can't just pop the fuck up whenever you feel like it and expect to get some mothafucking ass."

"Aww, girl, cut the games. You know you miss it."

"Nah, nigga. Run me that mothafucking money you owe me. That's what I'm missing."

Jamaal chuckled, clearly amused by my feistiness. He always told me my mouth was too smart for a soft nigga. "You real funny, you know that shit." He smiled, revealing his deep set of dimples. I always told him he reminded me of Juelz Santana but with dreads. Jamaal wasn't shit half the time, but the man was unquestionably fine. He was also trouble.

Eyeing the fresh fit and jewelry he had on, I quickly realized that he wasn't the same broke nigga I fell in love with. Everything was designer from the Versace shades perched on top of his head to the matching sneakers on his feet.

"You standing here looking like new money and shit, where my mothafucking cut at?" I asked.

"Man, calm down with all that shit, girl. Why you think I'm here?" Jamaal pulled off his Louis Vuitton backpack and handed it to me. "Real niggas do real shit."

After unzipping the bag, I eagerly peeked inside. Gasping in shock, I covered my mouth and looked up at Jamaal. There was a shitload of money in the backpack, each stack bundled tightly and labeled $10,000. If I had to guess, I'd say there was at least half a million present and accounted for.

"Damn, Jamaal. Where the hell did you get this kind of cash?"

"The details ain't important."

"Jamaal, I—are you for real? Boy, do not fucking play with me!" He only owed me $2,000 but I would've gladly taken all the money if he really was giving it to me. "I can have all of this? Are you serious? Are you fucking serious?"

"Dead ass."

"Jamaal...Oh my God! This is fucking incredible! Thank you! Thank you! Thank you God knows I really need this money! Oh my God!" Snatching out a single stack, I made it rain on my gotdamn self.

"Wait a minute, bitch...I'mma need you to calm the fuck down. Now there *is* one catch."

I sucked my teeth and blew out air. "Oh, boy, here we go." My mama said if something seemed too good to be true it probably was. "There's always a fucking catch when it comes to you. Well then...what is it?"

"Looks can be deceiving."

"What do you mean by that?"

"It looks real...but it's counterfeit."

"WHAT! Are you fucking serious? Boy, get the fuck outta here. What type of fool do you take me for?" Tossing the bag at his feet, I prepared to slam the door right in his damn face.

"Hol' up, hol' up...before you get so judgmental about it, I'mma need you to hear me out first." Jamaal quickly grabbed my elbow and turned me around.

"What else is there to say, Jamaal? You brought this fake ass money here thinking you was gon' get back in my good graces. I don't know who's stupider. You or me for believing you were really finna give me half a mil."

"But I guarantee every bill in that mufucka passes for the real thing," he said. "Go head. Pull out a band, thumb through it. You won't find a single defect. I put that on blood."

"And I'm supposed to believe that?"

"Look at it. Shit, that's all you gotta do."

Sighing deeply, I reached down, grabbed a stack of money from the bag, and looked closely at it. As sure as shit, it had the official blue band across every hundred. There wasn't a single imperfection in sight. The bills were absolutely flawless.

"You sure it'll pass for real?" I asked.

"Take that shit to the bank. You'll see."

"How could you be so sure? Have you tried to spend any of this money?"

"Go outside and look in the driveway."

Parked in front of the house was a brand new pearl white BMW convertible. It had a peanut butter wood grain interior, a fresh wax job, and custom Forgiatos rims that were at least six grand a piece. On the top of the hood was a huge, red bow.

"Fresh off the lot," he bragged. "The best for the best."

I hadn't even noticed the car until he pointed it out. "Oh, my God, Jamaal! You gotta be fucking kidding me! OH MY GOD! You bought me a car?!" I shouted with enthusiasm. "Hell yeah!" I was in complete shock and disbelief. I couldn't wait to floss and show out in my new car.

"Think of it as a peace offering." Jamaal pulled my face towards him. "Look, I know you think a nigga be on some bullshit. But now I got some shit that's gon' make everything right."

I wanted to believe he was being sincere, but the nigga had good ass penitentiary game. Jamaal was a habitual liar and a womanizer, who constantly sold dreams. "Jamaal...you know it's hard for me to trust you. You talking all this big shit now but you good for going MIA. Don't build me up just to tear me down—"

"Nah, we all the way to the top from here on out. No ceilings, baby. Enough of the games, a nigga tryin' to be on some real shit wit'chu."

"Yeah, I bet you are now that it's convenient for you. How do I know you ain't gon' be on that bullshit again?"

"Gimme a chance to prove it to you."

Because I felt myself getting emotional I quickly changed the topic. I hated for anyone—especially a man—to see me vulnerable. "Is this shit like...for real official? I mean like...*for real* for real? I won't run into any trouble spending this money, right? There won't be any problems?" I was still on probation so I had to tread very carefully.

"That money gon' spend itself."

"So I'm good?"

"You're great," Jamaal assured me. "Now can I get some of that mufuckin' tongue?"

"Nigga please. You ain't out the mothafucking doghouse yet."

"You still petty as fuck I see."

"Nah, I'm *real* as fuck."

I FELL IN LOVE WITH A REAL STREET THUG IS NOW AVAILABLE!

EXCERPT FROM "BACKPAGE" BY JADE JONES & CHASE MOORE

Royalty snorted and wiped his nose. Standing to his feet, he walked over towards the rail and looked down at the dance floor. His eyes scanned the massive crowd of club-goers until they finally settled on Lady.

Royalty lit an L as he watched her grind her colossal ass against Cap's mid-section. Lady's body was something fierce. She had a super tiny waist with massive thighs, and enough booty to donate to the less fortunate. A chocolate Keyshia Dior was what Royalty always told her she looked like.

Seeing Lady twerk on his homeboy had Royalty's dick rock hard. He had fucked her so many times that the sweet scent of her pussy was embedded in his memory. Without even trying, she managed to turn him on like no other.

Suddenly, Lady's dark-eyed gaze connected with Royalty's. Evidently, Allen wasn't the only one who liked to watch.

Royalty released the smoke through his nostrils as he continued to undress Lady with his eyes. His bad boy demeanor was what made her fall for him. That and the way he fucked her in the bedroom. Lady would have memories for a lifetime.

Royalty was an animal. His sexual appetite, insatiable. He was both aggressive and passionate when it came to sex. He made it his sole mission to fuck Lady into submission whenever they made love. He was the type of nigga that would choke you and pull your hair while telling you how much he loved you and needed you.

Lady smiled and blew a kiss to Royalty. She loved teasing him.

Royalty chuckled and pulled out his cellphone. He then sent a text message and patiently waited for her to receive it.

After feeling her phone vibrate, Lady pulled the iPhone out her black studded Louboutin clutch. Her eyes anxiously scanned Royalty's text which read: You gon' be my bitch 'til I expire.

"Tell that nigga wait his turn," Cap whispered in her ear as he held her from behind.

Lady slowly turned around and wrapped her arms around Cap's neck. For the moment, she decided to give him her undivided attention. "Don't tell me you're getting jealous," she teased.

Cap snickered. "Nah, none of that," he assured. "But, shit, if we gon' share yo' ass then he gon' have to learn to play fair."

Most people would never understand the four friends' kinship because society stressed that a regular couple consisted of two people. However, the quartet had made up their own standards, setting them apart from the rest.

Royalty and Cap were both Sweater and Lady's boyfriends. And Lady and Sweater were both of their girlfriends. Instead of the common two-way relationship, they had their own four-way thing going on. The friends lived together in a two-bedroom, two-bathroom home in Riverdale, and conducted their lives like every day normal couples.

Some nights Lady slept with Cap. Some nights Lady slept with Royalty. At the end of the day, they all had an understanding and more importantly they all trusted each other.

BACKPAGE IS NOW AVAILABLE!

Made in the USA
Middletown, DE
18 May 2022

65904102R00120